Langston Hughes

Young Black Poet

Illustrated by Robert Doremus

Langston Hughes

Young Black Poet

By Montrew Dunham

ALADDIN PAPERBACKS

First Aladdin Paperbacks edition August 1995

Aladdin Paperbacks
An imprint of Simon & Schuster Children's Publishing Division
1230 Avenue of the Americas
New York, NY 10020
Printed in the United States of America
10 9 8 7 6 5 4

Library of Congress Cataloging-in-Publication Data
Dunham, Montrew.
Langston Hughes : young black poet / by Montrew Dunham. — 1st Aladdin
Paperbacks ed.
p.   cm. — (Childhood of famous Americans)
Includes bibliographical references.
Summary: Focuses on the early years of the well-known poet, Langston Hughes, whose writings reflect the everyday experiences of African Americans.
ISBN 0-689-71787-3
1. Hughes, Langston, 1902-1967—Biography—Juvenile literature.
2. Afro-American poets—20th century—Biography—Juvenile literature.
[1. Hughes, Langston, 1902-1967—Childhood and youth.   2. Poets, American.
3. Afro-Americans—Biography.]   I. Title.   II. Series: Childhood of famous
Americans series.
PS3515.U274Z63   1995
818'.5209—dc20
[B]   93-21128

To Albert Howard Goetz

The author is deeply grateful to the following: Mrs. Dorothy L. Heim, Librarian, Central Junior High School, Cleveland, Ohio; Lester D. Plotner, Superintendent, School District 27, Lincoln, Illinois; Mrs. A. L. Gulup of Lincoln, Illinois; Mrs. Florence Kelley Martin of New Holland, Illinois; Mrs. Roy H. Johnson of Lincoln, Illinois; Jay W. Beswick, Cleveland Public Library; Dot E. Taylor, Kansas State Library; Mrs. Ehlert, Lawrence (Kansas) Free Library; and Mrs. Amy Ogden of the Downers Grove (Illinois) Public Library.

Quotations from "Minstrel Man," "The Negro Speaks of Rivers," "The Weary Blues," "Dreams," "Dream Variations," and "Daybreak in Alabama" are reprinted by permission of Alfred A. Knopf, Inc. Those from "Evening Air Blues" and "Troubled Island" are reprinted by permission of Harold Ober Associates, Inc. The quotation on page 188 is reprinted from Langston Hughes: A Biography by Milton Meltzer, copyright 1968 by Milton Meltzer, with permission of the publisher, Thomas Y. Crowell Company, Inc.

Illustrations

Full pages

Numerous smaller illustrations

Contents

★ # Langston Hughes

Young Black Poet

Lions and Tigers

ONE MORNING in Topeka, Kansas, young Langston Hughes slowly opened his eyes. He stretched his arms and legs and looked around the room, but all he could see were little bands of sunlight around the edges of the window shade. He and his mother lived in a large tenement building in Topeka. Already he could tell from the emptiness of the apartment that his mother had left for her day's work. She worked as a stenographer for a black attorney in Topeka.

With a bounce Langston rolled out of bed and pulled on his pants. From the sunlight outside, he felt sure it would be a good day. He ran over and put up a blind. In the foreground he noticed the big shadow of the tenement building. In the distance he could see the gleaming dome of the Kansas State Capitol Building.

His mother had left bread and milk on the table for his breakfast. As he chewed on a slice of bread, he thought of the household chores which she expected him to do. First, he would have to get a supply of kindling for the stove. He looked over at the black pot-bellied stove at one side of the room. This stove kept their room warm in the wintertime, but now it was used only for cooking.

He went over behind the stove and got out a gunny sack which he planned to fill with kindling. Then he went out the door, through the hall and down the stairway to the outside. "Good morning, Lang," called Mr. Johnson from his plumbing shop on the first floor. Most people in the building called him "Lang."

"Hi!" answered Langston, poking his head through the door of the shop. He liked the odors that came from the shop.

"Where are you going with that big bag?" asked Mr. Johnson. "Are you going out again to look for kindling?"

"Yes, I'm going down the alley to get kindling for our stove," answered Langston, starting on with the bag.

Langston loved to go down the back alleys of Topeka. Somehow they seemed more interesting than the streets. On either side there were picket fences loaded with flowers in back of people's houses. Also there were back walls of small business buildings, broken by back doors and windows. Outside the back doors there were piles of various kinds of trash which the businesses had discarded.

Langston went from trash pile to trash pile and picked up small pieces of wood and thick cardboard from discarded boxes. He put them carefully into the big bag and pushed them down tightly. Soon he had the bag filled.

Suddenly he noticed a huge crate at one of the back doors. He crawled into the crate and imagined it was somewhat like a cave. As he rested inside, he imagined how much fun it would be to live in a cave.

While he was resting in the crate, he noticed some ants scurrying through the sand in a low spot in the alley. The ants marched along steadily in a neat tiny row, one after another. They were headed for a small sand mound near one corner of the crate.

Langston crawled out of the crate and squatted down to watch the ants better. Soon he picked up a stick and shoved a little pile of dirt into their path. Then much to his astonishment, he noted that they merely walked around the pile of dirt and went on to their mound.

Young Langston wondered how the ants knew where they wanted to go. Of course, he knew where he wanted to go, but he was a boy who could think. He was puzzled because he doubted whether tiny ants could think.

Within a few minutes he picked up his bag of kindling and hurried back home. He waved at Mr. Johnson in the plumbing shop as he started to drag the bag of kindling up the steps. Once he reached the apartment he placed the bag neatly behind the stove.

Moments later he decided to call on Mr. Conrad, an architect who had an apartment nearby on the same floor. Mr. Conrad was sitting in a big chair by the window. He seemed to be very pleased to see Langston and called out to him, "Come here, Lang. I have a picture I would like to show you."

When Langston reached his side, he pointed to a picture of a large red-brick building. "I drew the plans for this building and actually constructed the building nearly twenty years ago," he continued. "Would you like to see what the plans for the building looked like?" Without waiting for Langston to answer, he reached under the table beside him and brought out a sheaf of blueprints.

"When you draw plans, do you always put up the buildings, too?" asked Langston.

"No, I usually just draw the plans and leave it to other persons to put up the buildings," replied Mr. Conrad.

He spread out the blueprints on the tall drafting board where he did most of his work. Langston crawled up on the high stool in front of the drafting board so that he could see well. Then Mr. Conrad pointed to the fine spidery white lines on several of the blueprints and told Langston what they meant.

After Langston finished looking at the blueprints, he went back to his apartment to eat the lunch which his mother had left for him. He got out a corn cake and placed it on a plate on the table. Then he got out a big jar and poured brown gooey molasses all over the cake. His mouth watered as he watched the thick molasses spread over the cake. Finally he picked up the cake in his hands and gobbled it down. As he ate it, he sipped on a glass of milk.

When he finished eating, his fingers were so sticky that they stuck together. He tried to pull them apart, but they went right back together again. Finally he poured some water in a wash-bowl and washed them carefully to get rid of the sticky coating. Then he shook off the water and started to wipe them quickly down the front of his shirt.

By now he was ready to call on another friend in the building. This time he ran down the hall to call on Mr. Jones, an artist who specialized in drawing and painting wild animals. Nearly every day he went to watch Mr. Jones daub brilliant colors on a canvas to make wild animals almost come to life.

Today as usual Mr. Jones smiled when he saw Langston slip into the room, but he didn't stop working. Instead he proceeded to spread great globs of vivid paint on the canvas. Then with a swish of his brush in one final stroke, he turned to Langston and said, "Well, here it is. What do you think of it?"

Langston could scarcely believe his eyes. "That big lion makes me afraid," he said. "He looks like he could jump right down on me."

"Well, he had better not jump down on you," laughed Mr. Jones. "Besides, it's time for you to go home to meet your mother. She'll be coming from the office almost any minute now."

Langston could scarcely believe that the afternoon was nearly over. As he ran down the hall, he heard his mother's footsteps coming up the stairs. "Hello, Mama," he called. "I'm coming to meet you."

After they reached the apartment, Langston's mother carefully removed the neat dark dress which she was wearing and put it away in a closet. Then she put on a loose, more comfortable cotton dress. Minutes later she started to get supper for herself and Langston and soon they sat down to eat.

After supper she took Langston to a public library a few blocks away. Along the way he started to walk on the narrow curbing at the edge of the pavement. Carefully he put one foot ahead of the other to balance himself on the curbing. Faster and faster he went, trying to keep up with his mother. Finally he stumbled and slid off into the grimy dirt beside her. "Oh, come on, Langston," she scolded as she reached down and pulled him to his feet.

Shamefully Langston looked down at his pants covered with dust. He brushed off the dust with his hands and thoughtlessly rubbed his hands on his face. His mother looked at him and took a deep breath when she discovered streaks of dirt on his face. She pulled a clean handkerchief from her dress pocket and rubbed his face to remove the dirt. Then she sighed as she looked at her dirty handkerchief.

When they entered the library, Langston's mother led the way to a table in a dark, silent room filled with books. "Wait here at this table until I return," she whispered.

Obediently Langston sat down quietly and started to wait. Curiously he looked around at the many shelves crammed with books. Suddenly a tall, pleasant librarian came walking up to the table. She smiled and laid an attractive book on the table before him. "Would you like to look at this book while you wait?" she asked.

Langston smiled shyly as he took the book and the librarian smiled back. He turned the pages slowly to look at pictures of a beautiful country. Before long his mother returned and explained that the book told about Mexico, the country where his father was living. He couldn't remember his father, but he imagined that he was a big bronze cowboy on a ranch in Mexico.

That evening as Langston walked home from the library with his mother, she said, "Langston, on Monday you will start to school. I have made arrangements for you to attend the Harrison Street School."

At this announcement, Langston felt a sudden rush of joy. He wondered what the school would be like. He wondered whether it would be like the library with stacks of books and whether the teachers in the school would be pleasant like the librarians.

In the fall of 1907 Langston started at the

all-white Harrison Street School. His mother had obtained special permission for him to go there rather than attend the all-Negro school on the other side of town. She had even gone to the members of the school board in Topeka to get this special permission.

On Monday Langston's mother took him to the Harrison Street School. At first he was frightened when he saw all the boys and girls, but not for long. The first-grade teacher smiled, took him by the hand, and led him to an empty desk. She patted him on the back and told him she was glad to have him in her class.

Langston liked the school and thought it was almost as nice as the library. Most of the boys and girls were friendly with him even though he was black. He especially liked a boy named Joey, who sat next to him. Soon he and Joey became very close friends.

All the teachers in the school were friendly

to Langston except one of the upper-grade teachers. Often she folded her arms and stared at him as if he didn't belong there. One day he overheard her say to another teacher, "I don't know why we have to have a colored child here at the Harrison Street School!"

Some of the older pupils heard the teacher, and they turned to stare at Langston. He saw them looking and felt uncomfortable but ran on to play. He couldn't understand why they didn't seem to like him.

That afternoon as he was walking home from school, he suddenly heard a rock whizz past his head. He turned to look and saw three older boys standing behind him with rocks in their hands. "Yah, colored boy," one of them shouted, "why don't you go to your own school?"

Langston was scared and shocked. He didn't understand what the boys meant. He thought that the Harrison Street School was his own

school because it was the nearest to his home. One of the boys wound up to throw another rock and Langston started to run. He was so frightened that his legs would hardly carry him. As he ran around the corner, he nearly bumped into Joey. "Hold it, Langston," cried Joey, throwing out his arm to protect himself.

When Joey found out why Langston was running, he started to run along with him. He picked up a tin can and threw it at the boys. Then he picked up a rock and several other things to throw at them.

Before long the older boys gave up the chase, and Joey and Langston stopped running. When they felt safe again, they sat down to rest. "Thanks, Joey, for helping me," said Langston. "You are a real friend."

"How come those big guys were trying to scare you?" asked Joey curiously.

Langston didn't know what to say, so he just

shrugged his shoulders. He scrambled to his feet and asked, "How would you like to come home with me this afternoon? Then I'll show you some lions and tigers."

"Lions and tigers!" exclaimed Joey. "Do you have wild animals at your house?"

"Come on and let me show you," said Langston, breaking into a grin.

The boys ran until they came to the tenement building where Langston lived. They climbed the stairs and Langston led the way down the hall to Mr. Jones' apartment. Eagerly he knocked on the door. "Who is there?" called Mr. Jones.

"I am a schoolboy," replied Langston. "May I bring a friend of mine inside to see your lions and tigers?" He could hear the faint sound of Mr. Jones' chuckle from within.

"Of course, come in!" called the artist as he kept right on painting.

Both boys entered the apartment with Joey being careful to stay behind Langston. He looked carefully from side to side and listened for animal sounds. Finally Langston pointed to an enormous painting hanging from a wall, which showed two buff-colored lions crouching as if ready to leap. Then he pointed to another painting of tawny, striped tigers with blazing eyes.

At first Joey just stood and looked. The animals seemed so real that he could scarcely believe they were paintings. Finally after he no longer felt afraid, he started to laugh.

Then Langston laughed, too.

To Mexico and Back

ONE SPRING DAY Langston hurried happily home from school. His thin coat failed to protect him from a cold gusty wind, but he didn't mind. The blue sky overhead was dotted with lazy white clouds. The yards along the streets were covered with fresh green grass. Even since yesterday the grass seemed greener than before.

When Langston entered the tenement house, he hurried rapidly along the hall. Just as he was ready to start up the stairs, he heard Mr. Johnson calling to him. "Lang," he said, holding a long envelope in his hand. "Here's a letter for your mama." The mailman regularly left mail with

Mr. Johnson for different people in the tenement building.

Langston took the long envelope and looked at it. In the center he identified his mother's name and address, "Mrs. Caroline Hughes, Topeka, Kansas," written in neat legible handwriting. In the upper right hand corner there was a beautiful foreign stamp.

A deep smile came over Langston's face. Then Mr. Johnson looked at him and said, "I suppose the letter is from your papa."

Langston nodded his head. "Yes," he said. "I can tell from the writing and the stamp."

Mr. Johnson smiled. He was pleased to see Langston happy. Somehow the lad always was excited about hearing from his father.

Langston rushed upstairs and laid the letter on the table for his mother. He could hardly wait for her to come home to read it to him. In a little while she would be there.

While he waited, he went over to check the fire in the pot-bellied stove. He placed several small pieces of wood over the red coals which were still glowing in the stove. He was careful to shove the pieces of wood all the way in. His mother had warned him not to leave pieces sticking out lest the ends burn off and catch the carpet on fire.

At last he sat down at the table to wait. He put his elbows on the table, rested his chin on his hands, and tried to imagine what his father in Mexico was like. As he sat with his eyes half closed, he could almost see his father astride a beautiful horse, galloping down a rugged mountainous road.

Finally he heard his mother's footsteps as she came up the stairs. He rushed out the door and ran down the hall to meet her. "Mama! Mama!" he shouted. "We have a letter from Papa!"

His mother smiled, but put her hand on his

shoulder and scolded him for being so noisy. "My land, Langston," she said, "stop making such a racket."

She walked over to the table and picked up the long envelope. She held it in her hand and looked closely at the writing and the stamp. Langston eagerly awaited for her to open it and start to read the letter inside.

Finally she slit the envelope across the top with a table knife. She took out the one sheet of paper inside and started to read. Quickly she moved her eyes from one side of the page to the other. Soon she began to frown and relaxed her arm so that her hand, still holding the letter, rested on the table. Then she looked down seriously at Langston and said, "Your father wants us to come to Mexico."

Langston's mouth dropped open in complete surprise. Finally he managed to ask, "May we go, Mama? May we go to Mexico?"

"I don't know," replied his mother. She looked at the letter again. "Your father wants us to come to live on his ranch."

Mrs. Hughes sat silently in deep thought for several minutes. Then suddenly she straightened up, lifted her head in a determined way, and said, "Yes, Langston, we're going to Mexico."

At once Langston was curious. He wondered what things would be like in Mexico. "Will I go to school there?" he asked.

His mother, still deep in thought, answered slowly, "We won't leave until you are out of school for the summer." She hesitated a moment and then added, "We'll ask Grandma Langston to go with us."

Grandma Langston was Mrs. Hughes' mother, who lived at Lawrence, Kansas. Langston loved his grandmother and was glad she, too, was going. She would help to look after him and to entertain him in Mexico.

His mother continued to talk as if she were thinking aloud. "We'll have a long, hard journey from Topeka, Kansas, to Mexico City," she said. "I'll have to pack our luggage and purchase our railroad tickets."

By now Langston wasn't quite certain whether he wanted to go to Mexico or not. Somehow, all of a sudden, it seemed like a faraway country. Besides, he would be sad about leaving the Harrison School and all his friends, both at school and in the neighborhood. "Why did Papa go to Mexico?" he asked.

Langston had heard this story before, but he liked to hear it over and over again. His mother looked off into space as if wondering what to say. Then she started off as she always did, "Your father, James Hughes, went to law school at the University of Kansas."

"Didn't you go to school there, too?" asked Langston, already knowing the answer.

His mother nodded. "Yes, that's where your father James and I first met," she replied. "He was a good student and was eager to become a successful lawyer. He wanted to practice law in Oklahoma, but first he had to pass the state bar examination there."

"Why?" asked Langston.

"All lawyers have to pass state bar examinations to practice law," his mother replied somewhat impatiently. Then she lifted her chin and said firmly, "When James went to Oklahoma, he was not allowed to take the examination."

"Why, Mama?" asked Langston. He still didn't understand this part of the story.

"They wouldn't let him take the examination because he was colored," explained his mother. "When this terrible thing happened, he was hurt and angry. That's why he left."

"Where did he go?" asked Langston.

"First he went to Cuba and then to Mexico.

34

He didn't really care where he would live. He just wanted to find a country where a colored man could get ahead in the world."

Langston felt puzzled. He couldn't understand why his father's color stopped him from taking an examination. Nor could he understand why he couldn't go to the movies because a sign said, "No Colored Allowed." Then he remembered how older white boys at school had chased him on his way home.

The train trip to Mexico was long and tiresome, but Langston thought it was exciting. He enjoyed curling up in the seat and listening to the rhythmic clicking of the wheels on the railroad tracks. He enjoyed looking out the window at the changing scenery in the countryside. He watched cows and other farm animals come into sight and then disappear. He watched forests come and go, often replaced by large areas of wastelands where little or nothing grew.

His mother and grandmother kept bringing out food to eat from mysterious boxes. Whenever he became tired, he crawled up in his mother's lap or leaned against his grandmother's shoulder. Then he quietly went to sleep.

Most of all he enjoyed getting a drink of water from a spigot on a water container at the end of the car. Time after time he walked down the aisle of the weaving train to get a drink. When he reached the end of the car, he braced his feet firmly to keep from falling. Then he held a little white paper cup under the spigot and pushed a button to make the water flow from the tank. When the cup was full, he carefully anchored himself and held the cup to his lips to drink the water.

One time as he was drinking, the train hurtled around a curve and caused him to spill water all over his shirt. "Shame on you, Langston, for being so careless," said his mother.

"Don't worry," said his grandmother, looking closely at his shirt. "It will soon dry."

Often when the train stopped at stations along the way, Langston and his mother and grandmother got off the train and walked up and down the station platforms. From these experiences he came to find that all railroad stations were much alike. Always people got off and on the train and workmen loaded and unloaded baggage near the front of the train.

At last the three weary travelers reached Mexico City, where they found Langston's father, James Hughes, waiting to meet them. Langston was surprised to find that his father was a short well-dressed businessman instead of the rugged horseman. At once his father rushed them off to a hotel for the night.

At the hotel Langston's father, mother, and grandmother had a long visit. Mr. Hughes told Langston's mother and grandmother about his success in Mexico City and about the ranch which was to be their home. The next morning he would take them on a long journey far into the country to the ranch.

Langston listened closely to the conversation and looked at his father in great wonder. He scarcely could imagine this well-dressed businessman owning a ranch. In fact, he couldn't imagine him even riding a horse.

That night after everybody had gone to sleep a terrible earthquake struck Mexico City. The buildings shook and many of them crashed and fell to the ground. The chandelier in Langston's room swung from the ceiling and a huge chest of drawers went sliding across the floor of his room. He jumped from his bed, frightened by the deafening noise. Half dazed, he began to scream in a panicky voice.

His parents came rushing into his room. His father grabbed him up in his arms and started

running down the stairs. His mother and grandmother followed, screaming with fright.

Finally they rushed out of the building and
crouched down together in the street. A huge
opera house across the street crumbled to the
ground with a mighty crash of falling bricks.

People everywhere ran about wildly, screaming in Spanish. Langston couldn't understand a word they were saying.

Countless numbers of black tarantulas came crawling from some of the collapsing buildings. One huge tarantula scrambled right past where Langston and the others were huddling. His mother was terribly frightened by the ugly creatures. "Oh, Lord, save us!" she cried.

The next morning after the earthquake, Langston's mother firmly announced, "I'm not going out to the ranch, and I'm not even going to stay in Mexico. Instead I'm going to catch the first train back to Kansas."

Langston's father couldn't understand her attitude. "You have nothing to fear here, because earthquakes are very unusual," he said. "Besides, I'm successful in business here. You'll like the ranch and will have a nice home there. You can go and come just as you please."

No matter what Langston's father said, his mother kept shaking her head. "I am going back to Kansas where we never have earthquakes," she said. "I can make a living there and will have nothing to fear."

"Maybe, but you also are going back to the color line," said Mr. Hughes bitterly. "Remember that we have no color line here."

Langston's mother still shook her head. So Langston, his mother, and his grandmother returned to Kansas. Langston didn't realize it at the time, but he wouldn't see his father again until he was seventeen years old.

Grandma Langston

AFTER LANGSTON and his mother and grandmother returned from Mexico, Langston stayed with his grandmother in Lawrence, Kansas, while his mother went elsewhere to find work. His grandmother owned a small cottage in a neighborhood where only white people lived. Sometimes she rented rooms to students who attended the University of Kansas, which was located only a few blocks away. She was a very proud woman who tried to make a living without doing housework or washing and ironing for white people, as most Negro women did.

At first Langston greatly missed his mother

and was very lonesome without her. One evening as he sat down at the supper table, he could hear the wind howling outside the cottage and felt more lonesome than ever.

Places for two people were set on the white, oilcloth-covered table, one for Langston and the other for his grandmother. A coal oil lamp, which sat on a nearby table, provided the only light in the room. Langston's grandmother dished up a bowlful of black-eyed peas and salt pork from a pot which had been simmering on the stove. She placed the bowl and a plate of left-over biscuit bread on the table.

Finally she sat down at the table across from Langston. Then both of them bowed their heads as she gave thanks. "Lord, bless this food for its intended use. Amen."

At first Langston merely sat staring at the food. His grandmother looked at him knowingly and said, "You miss your mother, don't you?"

Langston nodded and his grandmother added, "Don't fret. She will come back for you."

"I know," said Langston, trying to smile. "I only hope she will come soon."

Silently both Langston and his grandmother started to eat. As he looked across at his grandmother, he studied her copper-colored face, etched with fine wrinkles. He noted her straight, shiny black hair, which she wore tightly braided in a long twist around her head. Finally he looked over at her and said, "Grandma, you look like an Indian."

"Well, I am part Indian," she explained. "My grandmother was a Cherokee, and I could lay claim to Indian land, but I don't want the government to give me anything!"

By now Langston was listening so closely that he missed his mouth with a spoonful of beans and spilled them down the front of his shirt. "Be careful," scolded his grandmother. "Watch what you are doing. You'll have to wear that shirt to school tomorrow."

Langston looked down at his shirt and took a deep breath. His grandmother had made this shirt for him from a woman's discarded blouse. That very day at school some of the boys had teased him about wearing a woman's blouse. His grandmother looked at him and noted that his chin was trembling as if he was ready to cry. "Don't cry, Langston," she said.

Langston swallowed hard to hold back the tears and said, "I won't, Grandma."

"Well, don't," ordered his grandmother. "It never helps to cry."

Langston's grandmother wondered why he was upset. At last he told her how the boys had teased him about wearing a woman's blouse. She straightened up and looked at him with black glistening eyes. "It isn't what you wear but what you are that counts!" she declared.

That evening his grandmother got out a copy of a thin Negro magazine, called *The Crisis*. She sat down to read by the light of the coal oil lamp, which stood on the table. As she read aloud, Langston stood back of her and looked at the pictures. "This magazine is important because it wants Negroes to have equal rights with others," she said.

Langston had a number of questions that he wanted to ask. "Grandma," he said, "were you ever a slave?" He couldn't imagine his grandmother ever having been owned by anybody.

"No, Langston," she replied. "I was born free, and so was my father."

"Tell me about him," pleaded Langston.

He sat down by the rocking chair where she was sitting and leaned against her skirt, prepared to listen. Then she explained how her father had been a free man and a stonemason in Fayetteville, North Carolina. He had taught many slaves how to become stonemasons, if they ever became free. Often he had helped them to escape to freedom in the North by means of the Underground Railroad.

At this point Langston interrupted his grandmother for more information. "Just what was the Underground Railroad?" he asked.

"The Underground Railroad was a secret setup for helping slaves escape to the northern United States and Canada," replied his grandmother. "There were stations along the way where the Negroes could secure food and lodging. Your grandfather, Charles Langston, helped to run one of the stations. After the War between the States his brother, John Mercer Langston, was elected to the United States Congress. Then he was appointed United States Minister to Haiti and afterwards became dean of the first law school at Howard University."

The hour was getting late, but Langston

wanted his grandmother to keep on telling him stories about freeing the slaves. He especially wanted to hear her tell him about John Brown. "Please tell me how John Brown tried to help free the slaves," he said. "Who was he and what did he do for them?"

"Well," said his grandmother, lifting her head proudly, "John Brown was a white man who was born and raised in the East but later came to Kansas to live. He was an abolitionist who believed that something drastic should be done to free the slaves. He fought strenuously for the freedom of slaves right here in Kansas. Finally he came to believe that if he could take a bold step to help free the slaves, they would rise up in a revolt against their masters."

"What bold step did he take?" asked Langston, looking up into his grandmother's face.

"He organized a small group of men to start some kind of uprising in the South," she said.

"Eighteen men volunteered to join him, thirteen white men and five Negroes. One of the Negroes was my first husband, Sheridan Leary. John Brown took these men to Harpers Ferry, Virginia, where they seized a United States arsenal to get weapons for fighting. They hoped that the slaves nearby would desert their masters and come to join them in the uprising."

"Did they come?" asked Langston anxiously.

"No, the United States army took the arsenal back before the slaves could get started," replied his grandmother. "John Brown was captured and later hanged for treason. My husband, Sheridan Leary, was struck down by bullets and killed. As he lay dying, he removed this shawl from his shoulders and asked that it be returned to me." She held up the shawl so that Langston could see the bullet holes.

A few days after Langston's grandmother had told him about John Brown, she received a special letter from Theodore Roosevelt, President of the United States. This letter, which was written in fine, flowery handwriting, invited her to attend a meeting at Ossawatomie, Kansas, to honor John Brown. She was invited to attend as the last surviving widow of the men who had lost their lives with John Brown.

At the meeting in Ossawatomie Langston sat on the edge of a folding chair. Proudly he watched Theodore Roosevelt, President of the United States, lead his grandmother up the steps to the speaker's platform. Then he watched the President bestow special honors on her in memory of her first husband, Sheridan Leary.

Langston felt very proud as he sat and watched his grandmother on the platform with President Roosevelt. This was one of the most exciting days he had ever spent in his life. He wished it could go on forever because it was so different from many things in real life.

A year or so later Langston's grandmother took him to hear a famous Negro scientist, Booker T. Washington, speak at the University of Kansas. He was very much impressed with this prominent Negro and hoped that he, too, might become an important Negro.

Evening after evening while Langston lived with his grandmother, he sat by her chair and begged her to tell him interesting stories of the past. One evening after he had listened to several stories, he suddenly said, "Now, Grandma, tell me about going to college."

"Well," she said proudly, her black eyes shining brightly as she talked, "when I was a young lady, I attended Oberlin College in Ohio. I was the first Negro woman to be accepted at this all-white college. Both your father and mother went to the University of Kansas, right here in Lawrence. Now someday you must get a college education, too. You'll need to prepare yourself so you can amount to something worthwhile in the world."

Langston was too overwhelmed to speak. Soon the coal oil lamp on the table flickered and went out. Then his grandmother arose calmly from her chair and said, "When the light goes out, it's time to go to bed."

While living with his grandmother, Langston became an avid reader. Each summer he spent many hours reading in the nearby library, and he constantly carried books home to read. Then at home he stretched out in the shade of a tree and became carried away by the make-believe situations portrayed by the authors.

Most books, written in beautiful language, seemed to picture people in some kind of trouble. Then in the end the people seemed to be relieved of trouble. The mortgage was always paid or other similar good things happened. All this seemed strange to Langston, because he had come to feel that in real life somehow things never seemed to turn out right. The mortgage on his grandmother's home never was paid off, nor did other fortunate things happen.

One evening after supper Langston and his grandmother went outside to sit on the porch. His grandmother sat in her rocking chair as usual and Langston sat on the steps. He almost fell off the steps when the mortgage man brushed past him and said, "Good evening, Mrs. Langston. I have come for your mortgage money."

As Langston heard these words, he felt a tremor of fear. He wondered what his grandmother would do, because he knew that she didn't have enough money to make the payment. He watched and listened closely.

His grandmother arose in fine regal manner from her chair and started for the front door of the house. She completely ignored the man until she reached the door. Then she abruptly turned and said coldly, "Mr. Mortgage Man, I'll thank you to come back sometime tomorrow."

Langston lived with his grandmother for several years. Constantly throughout this period of time she was good to him and gave him a good home. She taught him many lessons which he remembered throughout life. Most of all she taught him to be proud that he was a Negro. She encouraged him to go to school and to read many books. She inspired him to want to make something of himself in the world after he grew up.

Aunt and Uncle Reed

ONE MORNING when Langston was twelve years old, his grandmother stayed in bed and said that she didn't feel well. She grew steadily worse and died before he could realize what was happening. Then the neighbors came in and everything about the house seemed strange and different.

Langston didn't cry, even though he felt sad over his grandmother's death. Somehow he had learned from her stories how useless it was to cry. His mother came to the funeral but had to leave right after the services to go back to work. "I'll send for you as soon as I possibly can," she said. He felt sure that she would.

After the funeral, Langston went to stay with two of his grandmother's friends, Auntie and Uncle Reed, in Lawrence. He thought that they were the best people in the world to take him in. They lived in a little white house with no mortgage to worry about.

That first night Langston felt very lonely as he lay in the strange feather bed and tried to sleep. He kept thinking of the funeral and could scarcely believe that his grandmother was gone. Every now and then he heard the dismal whistle of trains on the Santa Fe Railroad a short distance away.

He tried hard to lie still in the big strange bed but kept turning from one side to the other. All the while he tried hard to hold back hot salty tears in his eyes, because his grandmother wouldn't want him to cry.

Uncle Reed worked as a ditch digger for the city of Lawrence. He and Auntie Reed kept cows and chickens and sold milk and eggs to their neighbors. They let Langston help to take care of the cows and chickens.

Late one afternoon after Langston had driven the cows to pasture, he walked over to the railroad track. This was the first time he had gone there, even though he lived in the Reed home nearby. He sat down on a bank a safe distance away, hoping that a train soon would come rolling by. Before long he heard the shrill wail of a steam whistle cut the air.

Excitedly he squinted into the western setting sun. Far off in the distance he could see a freight train coming around a curve in the track. The puffs of smoke from the locomotive left a dusty trail that almost hid the train. It seemed almost as if the train were hurrying along trying to get away from the smoke.

Langston leaped to his feet to watch the freight train pass where he was waiting. He

waved to the engineer and fireman in the locomotive and to the other members of the crew in
the caboose. Then he watched the train highball
its way eastward with its wheels going clickety-
clack over the steel rails.

Langston knew that this train was bound for
Chicago. He had heard of Chicago and come to
think that it was an exciting place. Then, as he
sadly turned to leave, he wondered whether he
ever would have a chance to go to Chicago.

Back at the Reed home Uncle Reed sat in a
rocking chair in the kitchen, placidly smoking
his pipe. Auntie Reed was busy putting food on
the table for supper. She smiled as Langston
came in the door. "Scrub your hands, boy," she
said. "Supper is ready."

Langston hurriedly washed his hands and sat
down at the table. Auntie Reed had cooked a
wonderful supper of salt pork with greens and
corn dumplings. The steam curled up from the

dish and its fragrance completely filled the air. There were dishes of fresh peas and green onions from the garden. At each place there was a glass of cold milk to drink.

Somehow Auntie Reed's supper tonight seemed more appetizing than ever. Finally she brought out apple dumplings covered with butter sauce for dessert. Langston ate and ate until he felt full clear up to his chin.

Uncle and Auntie Reed were very good to Langston and tried to make him feel at home with them. Yet for all their goodness, he felt somewhat like a passed-around boy. Continuously he wished his mother would send for him.

On Sundays Auntie Reed dressed up in her best clothes and went to church. Always she made Langston go with her. Every Saturday night he had to take a hot bath in the kitchen. Then every Sunday morning he had to put on clean clothes and brush his hair down with oil.

Uncle Reed never went to church. Every Sunday morning he washed his overalls in a boiling pot over a hot fire in the backyard. Then while his overalls dried, he sat down in the shade of a grape arbor to smoke his pipe.

Auntie Reed never even looked in Uncle Reed's direction as she started to church. Always, however, Langston looked back and smiled. He thought that Uncle Reed was just as good as Auntie Reed even though he didn't go to church.

Late one afternoon a severe wind and rain storm, commonly called a cyclone, hit the city. Ever since noon Langston had been stretched out on the floor of the sitting room reading a book. Little by little it became so dark that he no longer could see to read.

Auntie Reed became alarmed at the approaching storm. Langston clambered to his feet and followed her closely to the door. "There's a bad storm coming out of the west," she said. "The whole earth is covered with darkness."

A sooty black cloud could be seen rolling rapidly out of the western sky. The earth seemed to be glowing with an eerie greenish light. The air had an unnatural stillness. Not a leaf stirred on the maple tree in the front yard. A chicken scuttled across the yard and dashed into the chicken house. "It looks like a cyclone coming," said Auntie Reed.

Langston had heard about cyclones, but had never seen one before. He had learned that people should seek safety in basements when cyclones approached. "Should we go to a basement somewhere?" he asked.

There was no basement in the Reed home. Auntie Reed's brown face folded into wrinkles as she answered, "I think we should, Langston. Let's go next door."

Suddenly a high wind began to tear through

the yard. It picked up particles of dirt and dust and swirled them through the air. Suddenly Langston spotted a giant black funnel cloud moving toward them in the sky. "Look, Auntie Reed! Look!" he cried in a frantic tone of voice. "There comes the cyclone!"

"Oh, my land! It's almost here!" she cried, grabbing Langston's hand. "Let's go to Morgans' basement as fast as we can."

Auntie Reed and Langston stepped out on the front porch. Suddenly they heard a deafening roar which seemed to shake everything around them. They rushed back into the house and moments later heard a creaking, crashing sound outside. Then they looked out and saw the front porch being carried away by the wind. They watched it sail through the air until it was completely swallowed up by the storm.

At first both Auntie Reed and Langston were speechless. As soon as they regained their wits, they tried to close the front door to shut out the storm. Finally they managed to push it shut. Then Auntie Reed sank down on the floor with her back to the wall and moaned, "My Lord, what a storm! What a storm!"

She pulled Langston down beside her and put

her arm around him. Then they huddled together on the floor and listened to the crackling of limbs being torn from the tree in the yard. Suddenly Auntie Reed happened to think of Uncle Reed, who still hadn't come home from work. "Oh, I wonder where he is?" she said. "I surely hope he has found shelter somewhere."

As she spoke, a mighty thrust of jagged lightning split the sky, and the storm seemed to become worse than ever. Auntie Reed prayed for everyone's safety, especially for the safety of Uncle Reed. Langston leaned closely against her and trembled from fear.

Minutes later the storm passed on and the sun came out for a beautiful clear sunset. The wind quieted down and the air seemed fresh and calm. Auntie Reed and Langston put on their boots and went outside to find out how much damage the storm had done. Almost immediately they saw Uncle Reed walking calmly toward the house. As he came near, he paused to look at the scars on the house where the porch had been. "That porch surely was pulled off mighty clean," he said. "You're lucky not to have been hurt."

Auntie Reed tossed her head to one side as if somewhat amazed. "I'm glad you are safe," she said. "I was praying for you."

Langston sloshed through the muddy puddles to discover damage which the cyclone had done. Soon as he looked about, he saw a rainbow far away in the sky. "Oh, look at that beautiful rainbow," he cried.

Both Uncle Reed and Auntie Reed looked at the rainbow. Uncle Reed lifted his arm and traced the rainbow from end to end. "It extends across the heavens to the pot of gold," he said.

Auntie Reed smiled and nodded her head in agreement. "Yes, it's God's promise to keep us all safe from harm," she said.

Class Poet

LANGSTON ENJOYED living with the Reeds, but was happy when his mother finally sent for him to come and live with her. She had married again and was living in Lincoln, Illinois. This sounded like a good place to live because Lincoln wasn't far from Chicago.

In Lincoln Langston's mother and stepfather lived in a nice little house on a tree-shaded street. His stepfather, Homer Clark, went off to work every morning. His mother stayed at home and did the washing, ironing, and cooking for the family. Months later she had a baby boy, whom she named Kit. Now Langston was extremely happy. For the first time in his life he felt that he was part of a real family. He wasn't a passed-around boy any more.

Soon he came to know several boys about his age in the neighborhood. Two of his favorite friends were a sandy-haired boy named Jimmy and a dark brown boy named Tom. Jimmy and Tom spent many hours showing him the city.

Langston enrolled in the eighth grade at Central School in Lincoln. His favorite teacher was Miss Ethel Welch, who led him to study hard to be a good pupil. Usually when the other pupils in class couldn't answer a question, she called on him. Always he felt good when he could answer it correctly.

Miss Welch found many interesting books for Langston to read. Oftentimes he repaid her by staying after school to help her clean the schoolroom. He washed the blackboards, dusted the erasers, and even swept the floor for her. One time when he was helping her, she asked, "Do you like to live in Lincoln, Langston?"

"Oh, yes, Miss Welch," Langston replied. "I like to live in Lincoln and I especially enjoy going to school here."

"Well, we're very proud of Lincoln," added Miss Welch. "We're proud because it is the only town in the country which was named for Abraham Lincoln before he became famous."

"Did Abraham Lincoln ever live here?" asked Langston curiously.

"No," replied Miss Welch. "Lincoln was a circuit rider who rode around on horseback from town to town practicing law. He came to Postville, Illinois, regularly on his circuit to look after people's law business. A group of men in Postville decided to lay out a new town to the east along the railroad and they hired Lincoln to do the legal work for them."

"Then what happened?" asked Langston.

"After the new town was laid out," explained Miss Welch, "the men asked Lincoln to conduct a christening ceremony and to name the new town Lincoln after himself. Then Lincoln shook his head and said, 'Nothing by the name of Lincoln ever amounted to anything.' Finally, however, he took a watermelon from a wagonload of watermelons standing nearby and announced, 'I christen thee Lincoln.'"

"That's an interesting story," said Langston. "Now I know another reason why Lincoln is a fine place to live."

Langston's mother loved poetry and often recited poems at church and club programs. One time she recited the famous old poem, "The Mother of the Gracchi." This poem was the sad story of a mother, named Cornelia, who lived in Rome centuries ago. She had two sons who were to be taken away by cruel fate. Langston and his friend Jimmy took the parts of the two sons.

As always, Langston's mother started to read the lines in loud impressive tones. The audience was enchanted by her reading and listened intently. Soon Langston became bored by the reading and thought the lines sounded very foolish. When his mother started to read about the two sons, he began to roll his eyes as if he were in great distress. Then many people in the audience began to giggle.

Of course Langston's mother wondered why the people were giggling. She read more loudly to bring out Cornelia's tragic story, and Langston rolled his eyes more wildly than ever. Finally the audience broke into a roar of laughter.

Langston's mother kept right on reading, even though she was annoyed. Dramatically she clasped the two boys in her arms, begging heaven for mercy. Even in this climactic act, Langston kept rolling his eyes. At the end the audience applauded madly with laughter.

After the program was over, Langston's mother found out about his clowning. When they reached home she gave him a whipping which he always remembered. From then on, he never disturbed her reading again.

One day near the end of the school year at Central School the pupils in the eighth grade held a meeting to arrange for their graduation exercises. Miss Welch stood at the front of the room to conduct the meeting. "Whom shall we choose for class poet?" she asked.

A girl in the class raised her hand, and Miss Welch nodded permission for her to speak. "I suggest Langston Hughes," she said.

Miss Welch smiled and glanced in Langston's direction. She thought that Langston was an excellent choice for class poet. First, Negroes were supposed to have rhythm, and Langston was one of only two Negroes in the class. Second, he was an exceptionally good student.

72

"But Miss Welch, I've never written a poem," Langston protested, taking a deep breath.

Miss Welch nodded her head reassuringly and said, "That doesn't matter. There's always a first time for everything."

As class poet, Langston's first problem was to select a subject for his poem. Finally he decided to write about the teachers in the school and the pupils in his class. He would write a stanza about each of the eight teachers in the school, with an especially good stanza about Miss Welch. Then he would write another eight stanzas about the pupils in his class.

Langston worked hard to find the right words for his poem. He made long lists of words that rhymed. Time after time he stayed after school so that Miss Welch could help him.

Each night after supper at home, he sat at the kitchen table to work on his poem. He turned up the flame on the coal oil lamp and put down words or revised words that he already had written. The bugs buzzed around the lamp and every now and then he took an idle swat with his hand to drive them away. Thus he worked until finally his poem was completed.

The eighth-grade graduation exercises were held late in May, 1916, in the gymnasium at Central School. The eighth-grade chorus filed in and stood on the risers to sing a song of greeting. Langston and the others who were to speak took their places on the stage. He was frightened and felt his heart pounding as he clutched the poem in his hand.

The program started and suddenly it was time for Langston to read. He arose nervously and walked to the center of the stage. His knees shook and he wondered whether the audience could see them shaking. He looked out fearfully at the crowd of faces staring at him. At first when he tried to read, he couldn't utter a word.

Then, when he regained his voice, it sounded strange and unnatural. Soon, however, he recovered his courage and read the poem well.

Just as he had planned, in the first half of the poem he praised all the teachers at Central

School. In the second half he lauded the members of the 1916 graduating class. When he finished reading, the people in the audience applauded enthusiastically.

Langston felt pleased with this applause. He sat down and proceeded to enjoy the rest of the program. Some members of the class recited selections from Shakespeare and others played musical selections. Finally the president of the board of education handed diplomas to all members of the class.

That evening as Langston and his mother returned home, both of them were very proud and happy. Langston had graduated.

Off to Cleveland

AT THE TIME Langston graduated from Central School in Lincoln, his stepfather Homer Clark, was in Cleveland, Ohio, looking for work. Soon he sent for his family to come to Cleveland to live. Langston was sorry to leave his many friends in Lincoln, but he had no other choice. Now he would have to look for new friends to take their places.

When Langston and his mother and half-brother Kit reached Cleveland, his stepfather was waiting to meet them. At once he took them to an apartment which he had rented in a big house on the east side of town. He led the way up a front stairway to the second floor, and then up a narrower stairway to the third floor. Finally he opened the door of a small attic apartment with tiny windows looking out over the roof. "Is this where we are going to live?" asked Langston's mother in surprise.

Mr. Clark shook his head. "Rents here in Cleveland are very high," he explained.

"Surely not for this," said Langston's mother, glancing at the crowded quarters.

"Negroes in Cleveland have a hard time finding places to live," added her husband apologetically. "Most of them have to live in small apartments which white people have made by dividing up their houses. This apartment is part of an old house."

"Well, it's a terrible place to live," said Langston's mother. "Certainly we can find a better place somewhere else."

Langston went over to look out the windows.

78

He could see a long way across the city. In the distance he noticed black smoke belching from the tall chimneys of several factories.

Almost at once Langston liked Cleveland. He liked the noisy confusion of the city with people coming and going on the streets and sidewalks all hours of the day and night. He liked the friendliness of the people and soon became acquainted with many boys and girls in the neighborhood. Often they took him on long walks to show him other parts of the city. Soon he was glad that he had moved.

That September he entered Central High School in Cleveland. He felt very fortunate to be able to attend such a fine school. He liked both the teachers and the students in the school. The students were mostly Negroes, but in addition there were Poles, Russians, Hungarians, Italians, and Jews.

Langston's best friend was a Polish boy named

Sartur Andrzejewski, who sat next to him in an art class. One day Langston was supposed to make a poster, but he didn't know how to begin. "Just start like this," explained Sartur, taking a large sheet of paper and quickly outlining a human face in bold color.

Sartur made drawing look easy, but Langston still sat and looked at his blank paper. Finally the art teacher came and stood behind him. Quietly she said, "The only way to accomplish something is to get started. Then you just keep on working until you finish."

Slowly Langston started to sketch. He gradually gained confidence and soon was able to draw and paint along with the others. After he finished his poster, the art teacher examined it with approving eyes. "It's very appealing, Langston," she said. "Now you see how important it is to get started at something and to keep on working at it until you finish." From then on

Langston completed many assignments in art which at first he didn't think he could do.

One day Sartur said, "There's a new settlement house around the corner from where you live. Let's go over to see what it's like."

"All right," said Langston. "I've heard it is a kind of community center."

The two boys went to the settlement house, which was called Karamu, meaning a place of enjoyment in the Swahili language. There they mingled with many other young people, both Negro and white, from the neighborhood. Much to their surprise, they found that they could take free lessons in drawing and painting at the settlement house. Later they volunteered to teach drawing to some of the smaller children.

One evening, Sartur asked Langston to go home with him for dinner. At first Langston felt a little shy in the Polish home, but Sartur's mother and two younger sisters made him welcome. Sartur's mother had prepared supper and the air was filled with delicious odors. Soon his father came in from the mills and immediately called out, "What's for supper?" The whole family had a quaint and kindly way of living.

At once Sartur's mother carried large bowls of cabbage and heavy dumplings to the table. Then all the members of the family and Langston sat down to eat. Langston was particularly fond of the cabbage with its sweet-sour taste and took several helpings.

When the school year ended, Langston and his friends hunted jobs for the summer. Most of his friends found places to work in the neighborhood, but he was not so fortunate. Finally he obtained a job running a dumb waiter or freight elevator in a large department store downtown.

At about the same time Langston's stepfather became ill from working in the hot steel mill. He spent much time stretched out on the daybed

at home, struggling to get his breath. Finally his wife said, "Homer, you just can't work in that hot steel mill any longer. You'll have to find something else to do."

As soon as Mr. Clark felt well enough, he went job hunting again. Soon he found a job doing light work but received little pay. Hour after hour he sat at the kitchen table trying to figure out ways to stretch out his earnings enough to pay bills. "There is only one way," said Langston's mother. "I'll have to go to work, too. The neighbor woman downstairs will take care of Kit while I'm away."

Before long Langston's mother obtained a job in a nearby restaurant. Then both she and Langston brought home money to help pay the rent and other living expenses.

At the department store Langston had to move merchandise from the stockroom to various departments in the store. One day he delivered several bottles of perfume to the cosmetics counter. While he was putting the bottles on a shelf, he watched the saleslady wait on a lady customer standing at the counter.

The day was very hot, but the lady had a fur cape dangling loosely from her shoulders. She picked up a bottle of delicate perfume from the counter and held it up daintily in her hand. "How much is this bottle?" she asked.

"Fifty dollars, Madam," replied the saleslady graciously.

"Very well," said the lady without hesitation. "I'll take it."

Langston was stunned, but turned and walked away to continue his work. He could scarcely believe that anybody had enough money to spend fifty dollars for one bottle of perfume.

Working and Learning

WHEN SEPTEMBER came, Langston went back to Central High School, but his parents were still working hard to make enough money to pay their living expenses. He was sorry that he could no longer work to help them.

He thoroughly enjoyed his school work this year. Each morning he prepared to leave for school he looked forward to learning or doing something exciting. His favorite class was literature, where he first came to know the work of famous authors. Two other classes that he liked were geometry and world history.

In literature Langston spent many hours

reading poems written by Vachel Lindsay, Carl Sandburg, Amy Lowell, and Edgar Lee Masters. In particular he loved the rolling rhythm of Lindsay's poems and the forceful, down-to-earth quality of Sandburg's poems. Finally he was inspired to try writing poems of his own, based on the style of Sandburg.

One evening after school, Langston, his Polish friend Sartur, and a Jewish friend Nathan rushed along the street on their way home. Carelessly they almost bumped into a couple strolling along the sidewalk. The man turned and snarled, "Can't you niggers, polacks, and kikes watch where you're going?"

Langston was shocked by these words of prejudice and hatred. He felt a cold feeling of revulsion going through him, but his friends went right on walking and talking as if nothing had happened. Then he realized that tolerance rather than anger was the best policy.

The next summer Langston's stepfather and his mother gave up their apartment in Cleveland. His stepfather went out of town to look for a job and his mother obtained a job as a cook in Chicago. She was to work for a lady who owned a hat shop. Langston obtained a job as a delivery boy for the hat shop.

This change was very exciting to Langston. He remembered how he had watched Santa Fe trains pass through Lawrence, Kansas, on their way to Chicago. Also he remembered reading Carl Sandburg's poem "Chicago." Now he couldn't believe that he was going there.

His mother could afford to rent only one small room in a Negro district of the city. The building was dark and gloomy and filled with the odors of stale food. The two small windows in the room opened out on the tracks of the elevated railroad. Every few minutes elevated trains thundered by with a deafening roar.

Almost immediately Langston went out to explore one of the main streets in the Negro district. The street was lined with shops, restaurants, and cabarets. The sidewalks were crowded with people, many standing in little groups, laughing and talking. Children ran noisily here and there. One small child toddled along licking a giant chocolate ice cream cone.

One Sunday Langston took a long walk to see other parts of the city. He wandered from the Negro district into a white district, which seemed somewhat less crowded. The houses were set neatly in rows a little way back from the sidewalks. Behind the houses there were fenced-in yards, many with trees for shade. Most of the houses had starched lace curtains hanging at the front windows.

As Langston walked along, he noticed white people sitting on a few of the front porches. Most of the people, however, seemed to be con-

gregated in their back yards. There were very few persons walking along the streets.

Before long Langston thought that he heard footsteps behind him. He turned to look and found a large white boy almost at his heels followed by three other white boys. He stepped aside to let the boys pass, but they didn't go on. Instead the tall boy stared in Langston's face and snarled, "We don't allow niggers in this neighborhood!"

Langston felt a surge of panic at these unexpected words. Then suddenly all four boys started to beat and pound him with their fists. He tried to escape, but they kept blocking him. Finally one of them gave him a shove and said, "Now get out of here!"

By now Langston's heart was pounding and his knees felt wobbly, but he managed to start running. He kept running until he was certain that he was back in the Negro district again. For several days afterward he had a swollen jaw and two black eyes from the beating.

When the summer was over, Langston returned to Central High School in Cleveland, but his mother stayed on her job in Chicago. He had saved enough money to rent an inexpensive room in a house. He cooked his own meals, which consisted mostly of hotdogs and rice. Each night he read himself to sleep.

A few months later his stepfather Homer Clark returned to Cleveland to work, and his mother found a job working in a Cleveland restaurant. Then once more the family lived together in a Cleveland apartment.

Langston spent a very happy year in Central High School. His school work was exciting and he enjoyed associating with his many school friends. In his literature course he read the works of many classical and modern authors. He attended many social functions and was active in several school clubs. He wrote articles for a school paper called *The Belfry Owl* and helped to prepare the school yearbook.

One night at home he tried to read a story in French by Guy de Maupassant. He worked hard to make out the meaning of the story from the French words, many of which he had to look up in a French dictionary. Finally after many hours of deep study he managed to read the story through to the end.

Then once more he read the story for sheer enjoyment. This time he could sense the real meaning of the author's words. He could feel the chill of the winter cold, see the soft white snowflakes drifting down, and hear the metallic crunch of footsteps in the snow underfoot. He almost shivered with delight.

As he finished reading this story, he felt a strong urge to attempt to write something himself. He was eager to write about Negroes, to paint vivid pictures about them which people could read with understanding and feeling.

At this time he felt that he could write poems far more readily than stories. During the succeeding months he wrote many poems, but he was very shy about showing them to his friends. Instead he mailed most of them to magazines in New York, hoping to have them published.

Each time after he sent a poem to a magazine, he watched the mailbox very carefully for a reply. Then, sooner or later, he received the poem back with a printed slip rejecting it.

Mexico Again

ONE DAY near the end of the school year in Cleveland, Langston looked in the mailbox and unexpectedly found a letter from his father. He almost dropped his bundle of schoolbooks in amazement. This was the first time he had heard from his father since he had spent that frightening night in Mexico City many years before. Quickly he tore open the envelope and pulled out the single sheet of paper inside. Then he read hurriedly the following message:

My Dear Langston:
   I am going to New York for a few days on a business trip in June. On the way back I will

send you a telegram to meet me as the train comes through Cleveland. I want you to accompany me to Mexico for the summer.

Affectionately,

Your father, James N. Hughes

Langston hastened to show the unexpected letter to his mother. She read it carefully and placed it on the table, but failed to discuss it with him. Finally he said, "I probably should begin to get my things together."

"For what?" she exclaimed coldly. She looked cross and disapproving.

"To go to Mexico with my father," Langston replied, somewhat bewildered.

"Why should you go?" asked his mother. "What has he done for you all these years?"

Langston couldn't understand his mother's attitude toward his father. He pictured his father as an important businessman in Mexico City, who would help him to have an enjoyable summer. Already he could visualize the bright sunshine, rugged snow-capped mountains, and prickly cacti in this faraway country.

"I think he should go," said Langston's step-father. "It will be good for him."

Quietly Langston packed his few possessions in a small suitcase. He wanted to be sure to be ready when he received the telegram from his father. Then, when the telegram came several days later, he almost missed receiving it.

After Langston received the letter from his father, his family moved to another apartment with a new address. Langston went back to arrange with the former landlady to notify him when the telegram came. When he reached the house, he found the telegram stuck in the mailbox. Then he opened it and read:

Passing through ten-fifty tonight. Be ready. Board train at station.

James N. Hughes

Langston's heart rose in his throat. The telegram had been delivered the day before, and already he had missed his father. He had a feeling of complete helplessness.

After he regained his composure, he happened to think that possibly his father had gotten off the train and registered at a Cleveland hotel. He ran into the landlady's apartment, grabbed a telephone directory, and started to call the nearby Negro hotels. Soon he located a hotel only a short distance away where a man by the name of James N. Hughes was registered.

He rushed from the apartment and started to walk hurriedly toward the hotel. After he had gone a short way, he noticed a well-dressed short dark man striding rapidly in his direction. As they met they stared closely at each other and then looked back. "Are you Langston Hughes?" called the man.

"Yes," nodded Langston, looking closely at the man. "Are you my father?"

"Of course," replied the man brusquely. "Why weren't you at the train last night?"

"We moved and I didn't get your telegram until this morning," explained Langston.

"Just like niggers," sneered his father. "You're always moving. Are you ready to go?"

Following this conversation Langston felt uncomfortable. For a moment he was almost ready to change his mind about going. "Well, come on," ordered his father.

"All right," replied Langston, "but first I must tell my mother good-by."

He went into the restaurant where his mother was working, but she didn't even look at him. "Good-by," he said softly. "I'll be back at the end of the summer."

His mother didn't answer but went right on carrying dishes to the kitchen. He hated to leave when she was angry, but finally he had to because there was nothing else to do.

Hesitantly he went to get his suitcase and started to the railroad station with his father. Somehow by now he had a very strange feeling about his father. He wondered whether his mother was right in objecting to him going. Soon after he reached Mexico, he found out.

That summer was one of the most miserable summers Langston ever spent. He discovered that his father's sole purpose in life was to make and keep money. He practiced law, and he owned property in Mexico City and a big ranch in the hills. He was general manager of an American electric light company in Mexico. He loaned money to people and foreclosed on their mortgages when they couldn't pay. Most people in Mexico thought of him as a dark-skinned American, but few realized that he was a Negro.

James N. Hughes hated poor people. He was critical of anyone who didn't make money and improve his lot. He wanted Langston to come to

Mexico as soon as he finished high school so that he could start to make money, too.

When Langston and his father arrived in Mexico City, they stayed at the Grand Hotel. As soon as they had changed their clothes, they went to call on some of his father's rich friends. When they reached the house, an Indian servant opened the door and ushered them into a cool, dark foyer. In the parlor there were large statues around the walls. The people were pleasant, but Langston was glad to leave.

Langston hoped that he and his father would stay in Mexico City long enough for him to go sightseeing in the city. His father shook his head and said that they couldn't waste that much time. The next morning they boarded a train for Toluca, where his father was manager of the electric light company.

On the way to Toluca they rode in a hot dirty coach. All the seats were filled, and people stood elbow to elbow in the aisles. Many of them held big parcels under their arms, and there was scarcely room to move.

Along the way, the train wound up and around mountains. Finally when it approached Toluca, it descended into a beautiful valley with velvety green fields dotted with clear blue lakes. In the distance there was a majestic snow-capped volcano, La Nevada de Toluca. The air in the valley was fresh and invigorating, and the sun shone from a clear blue sky.

Langston's father lived in a low, white rambling one-story house, surrounded by a blue-white wall. At the front of the house there was a patio, but the grass and flowers round about had a strangely unkempt appearance. There were two servants in the house, a tall thin Mexican woman, who served as housekeeper, and a small Indian boy, named Maximiliano, who served as chore boy. Maximiliano came to take the luggage into the house and the Mexican woman hastily served a small lunch on the patio.

Early in the afternoon Langston's father took off on horseback for his ranch. Langston wanted to go with him, but his father refused to take him. "I can't take you because the roads are full of bandits," he said.

After his father left for the ranch, Langston felt very strange staying alone in the house with the two servants. Soon he discovered that his father paid them very little money, so he began to share his allowance with them. From then on they did everything possible to make him comfortable and happy.

Almost immediately Langston and Maximiliano became close friends. Maximiliano taught him how to ride a horse without a saddle or stirrups. Day after day they rode the dusty roads to the foothills of the snowcapped mountains.

Shortly after Langston's father returned from

the ranch, he decided that Langston should become a bookkeeper. He gave him long rows of figures and showed him exactly what to do with them. Then he coldly issued the command, "Now get started! Hurry up! Hurry up!"

Langston worked hard at bookkeeping, but he failed to satisfy his father. Always his father expected him to do more than he could. Repeatedly he told him to get more done.

James N. Hughes had boundless energy and worked at a tremendous pace. He expected all his helpers to work just as rapidly and hard as he did. For this reason he constantly spurred them on by saying, "Hurry up!"

The hot summer days went past, and Langston didn't hear from his mother. By now he understood why she couldn't be happy living with his father. He was homesick and lonely and began to feel sorry for himself.

Whenever he could spare the time, he took

long horseback rides. He rode out into the little villages where he was attracted by the churches. Each church had a beautiful white Spanish tower with great bells hanging in the turret.

One day in August, when Langston's father came home, he suddenly came to realize that Langston felt sad and lonely. "Ten days from now I'm going to Mexico City on business," he said. "How would you like to go along? Then you can see the summer bullfights and Xochimilco."

At first Langston was too surprised to answer. He had been in Mexico all summer and this was the first time that his father had offered to take him anywhere. Finally he managed to thank his father and to say that he would be delighted to go along. Moments later he hurried out to lie on the grass and to dream about the wonderful holiday he would have in Mexico City and the interesting sights he would see.

During the coming ten days Langston's father gave Langston a rough time in bookkeeping. Each day he gave him pages and pages of figures. Then he ordered, "Hurry up and get those figures done so I can check them. Hurry up." In addition he decided to teach Langston how to use the typewriter. Each evening after supper he gave him several exercises to type and ordered, "Now type those exercises a hundred times before you go to bed."

At last the day came for Langston and his father to leave for Mexico City. His father awakened him at 4:30 o'clock in the morning. "Hurry up and get dressed," he said.

Langston crawled out of bed, but somehow he didn't feel right. He managed to dress and reach the breakfast table, but was too sick to eat. All the while his father gulped his food down and shouted, "Hurry up!"

Suddenly Langston felt as if his stomach would turn inside out. His body shook and he broke out in a deep sweat. Everything around him seemed to be swirling round and round. Finally he got up and staggered back to bed.

Langston's father could readily see that he was seriously ill. He called a doctor who said that Langston should be taken to a hospital. Then he put Langston on a train and took him to a hospital in Mexico City. There Langston stayed in the hospital for nearly three weeks, recovering from his illness.

Early in September Langston climbed on a train to return to Cleveland. He had spent a full summer in Mexico with his father without seeing either a bullfight or Xochimilco. Now he fully understood why his mother had objected so strenuously to his coming here.

High School
Graduate

LANGSTON WAS glad to be back in Cleveland with his family. Both his mother and stepfather had to work hard to earn enough money to pay their rent and other living expenses. They lived in a small basement apartment which was all they could afford from their limited income.

At first Langston's mother suggested that he get a job to help support the family, but he wanted to go back to Central High School. He felt that he should finish high school before he started to work. His stepfather agreed. "Langston should finish his high school," he said. "He should go back to school."

Following this decision, Langston returned to school and spent an exciting year at Central High School. He studied hard and took part in many high school activities. He was a member of the track team and was chosen one of a group of editors to prepare the school yearbook.

During the school year Langston spent many hours writing poems, and near the end of the year he was elected class poet. He also spent much time at the Karamu Settlement House helping to work with the younger Negro children in the neighborhood.

One evening at a party Langston met a pretty little brownskin girl, named Susanna Jones. Shyly he introduced himself and sat down to talk with her. Much to his surprise, he found that even though she was seventeen years old, she only was attending junior high school. He couldn't understand why this intelligent girl wasn't farther along in school. Then she explained that she and her family had just moved to Cleveland from the South, where she had no opportunity to attend high school.

Langston and Susanna became close friends. She had big eyes and her voice was soft and gentle. Her skin was delicate, the color of rich chocolate. Sometimes she wore a red dress which Langston greatly admired. Finally he was moved to write a poem about her which started with the following lines:

> When Susanna Jones wears red
> Her face is like an ancient cameo
> Turned brown by the ages.

Langston placed this poetic tribute to Susanna in a notebook along with other poems which he had written. Sometimes he spent hours writing serious poems on subjects of special interest. At other times he merely jotted down verses or jingles that popped into his mind.

When graduation time came in June, Lang-

ston was filled with mixed feelings. He had spent four happy and challenging years at Central High School. Now he wondered what he would do next. As he marched down the aisle to receive his diploma, he looked at the serious faces of all his classmates. Then he knew that they, too, were wondering what they would do after they received their diplomas. Only a few could enter college because most parents couldn't afford to send their children to college.

Langston, like some of the others in his class, wanted to go to college. He realized, however, that the only way he would have this opportunity would be to pay his own way.

One day shortly after he graduated, he received a letter from his father asking him to come to Mexico to discuss his plans for the future. In the letter his father hinted vaguely about the possibility of going to college. Langston had no desire to go to Mexico again, yet he felt that by going he might have an opportunity to go to college. He sat down at the kitchen table and reread the letter several times. Finally he read it to his mother, but she merely kept on doing her work. He could tell by her looks and actions that she was greatly annoyed.

Langston shuddered as he thought about his last summer in Mexico. He wondered whether an opportunity to go to college would be worth all the hurry-up nagging he would have to take from his father. At last he put his feeling into words. "Mama," he said, "if I don't go to Mexico, I don't know how I'll ever get a chance to go to college."

His mother turned and faced him squarely. "We've had to work hard to send you to high school," she said. "Now it's time for you to go to work to help us out a little."

Langston kept right on trying to convince his mother. "I need to go to college so I can get a

114

good job and amount to something in life," he argued. "What kind of job do you think I can get now? Maybe I can become a porter or a bus boy, but what about my future?"

His mother sank wearily into the chair and merely repeated, "Now it's time for you to go to work to help us out a little."

Langston realized that his mother was very tired and felt sorry for her. Maybe he wasn't being fair to her by keeping on arguing about going to college. Then he remembered that both his mother and grandmother had gone to college. Finally he said, "Mama, you went to college, and Grandma was the first Negro woman to attend Oberlin College. Surely you know how important it is for me to go to college."

His mother said bitterly, "I suppose you are right, but just see how much good a college education has done for me."

At last Langston made arrangements to accept his father's invitation to come to Mexico. The day he was to leave, his mother went to work without bidding him good-by. The only person left at home was his little half-brother Kit, who watched closely as he packed his belongings in an old suitcase.

When he was ready to leave, he took Kit over to the neighbor woman who regularly looked after him while his mother was away. As he turned to leave, he swallowed hard and squeezed Kit's little hand. "Good-by, brother," he said. "I'll come back to see you."

"Good-by," said Kit. His round face was solemn and his eyes were filled with tears.

Langston left quickly. His throat felt tight and he still wondered whether he was doing the right thing. Only time would tell.

"I've Known Rivers"

THE DAY Langston left for Mexico, he half-heartedly boarded a train at the Cleveland railroad station. Haltingly he walked through the coach, swung his flimsy suitcase up to the rack, and sat down by a window. Now that he was actually started on his long trip, he greatly regretted he had decided to go.

As the train rolled out of the station, he leaned his head back on the seat and closed his eyes. The sound of the rhythmic clicking of the wheels on the railroad tracks sounded harsh and shallow to his ears. He thought of his father and his intense desire to make money.

117

Even though his father was successful in business, he never seemed to be happy and seldom, if ever, smiled. Strangely, he tried to stay away from Negroes and didn't want people to know that he himself was a Negro. He didn't like Negroes and didn't even like himself because he was a Negro.

Suddenly Langston opened his eyes and sat up straight as if to shake himself loose from all these thoughts about his father. He was a Negro and he wanted people to know that he was black. He thought of his many Negro friends and how he enjoyed being with them. He felt very sad about leaving them.

His memories turned to Negroes who had come to a soda fountain where he had worked for a while in Cleveland. He remembered how these Negroes had talked and laughed in spite of their problems and worries. To him Negroes were the gayest and bravest people in the world.

Even though they had to fight for many of their rights, they still could laugh and be happy.

After a while Langston became tired of sitting and began to feel hungry. He counted his money and found that he had enough to go to the diner to eat. Besides, he was going to see his father and soon would have no further need for money. Calmly he arose from his seat and walked from one lurching car to another toward the rear of the train. Finally he came to the diner, which was the last car on the train.

Inside the diner he noticed the attractive tables along each side of the car. All the tables were covered with sparkling white tablecloths. All of them were set with heavy silverware for four people to eat. All had heavy silver creamers and sugar bowls ready to use. Each table was decorated with a single red rose extending from a tall narrow vase.

The headwaiter seated Langston at one of the

tables and handed him an enormous menu. As Langston looked at the menu, he wondered how the chefs could prepare so many foods in such small quarters. Finally he selected what he could afford to order with his money.

"May I serve you, sir?" asked a Negro waiter, wearing a sparkling smile on his gleaming brown face. He seemed so cheerful and spoke so pleasantly that he made Langston almost completely forget his problems.

"I'd like a fruit cocktail, clam chowder, chef's salad, and pork chops," answered Langston, looking up from the menu.

The waiter wrote all the items down carefully on a card. Soon he returned and placed a large fruit cocktail on the table in front of Langston. Next he brought the clam chowder and finally the chef's salad and pork chops. Langston ate slowly, enjoying every bite.

While he still was eating his pork chops, he

noticed a white man staring at him from a table across the aisle. The man's constant staring made him feel restless and uneasy. At first he wondered whether the man was annoyed by his poor table manners, but soon he realized that the man was not only annoyed but angry. Finally the man jumped up from the table and blurted out, "You're a nigger, aren't you?"

With these words he brushed past Langston out of the diner. Almost without thinking, Langston started to laugh. He was amused because the man had become angry at Langston merely because he was eating in the diner. Langston knew that he had to laugh in order to keep from crying. At this moment there seemed to be a narrow line between laughing and crying.

The Negro waiter, standing at one side, had overheard the white man. Soon he returned to Langston's table to pick up some of the dirty dishes. He didn't say anything but noticed that

Langston was laughing. Then he shrugged his shoulders and started to laugh, too.

After dinner Langston retraced his way back through the train. As he walked through the cars, he wondered what would happen if he should run into the white man again. By now he had quit laughing and was thinking seriously about his unpleasant experience.

When Langston reached his seat, he sat down and looked out at the beautiful sunset. The rich orange-red rays of the sun seemed to add color to everything in sight. Just at that moment the train started to pull slowly over the long bridge across the Mississippi River.

As Langston looked down at the muddy water, he remembered how Abraham Lincoln had gone down the Mississippi on a raft to New Orleans. On that trip Lincoln had seen slavery at its worst. Possibly even then he had realized that slavery had to be abolished.

Soon Langston's thoughts turned to other rivers that had greatly influenced the lives of Negroes, especially ancient rivers of Asia and Africa. Hastily he pulled out an envelope and jotted down the title "A Negro Speaks of Rivers."

From then on he sat in deep thought, trying to put his feelings about rivers and Negroes into poetic form. He explained how certain ancient rivers, including the Euphrates in Asia and the Congo and Nile in Africa, had helped to determine the destiny of Negroes. He described the Mississippi as a singing river, when Abraham Lincoln had sailed down to New Orleans, but now as a muddy river whose water had just turned golden in the sunset.

Finally he concluded with these lines:

"I've known rivers,
Ancient, dusky rivers,
My soul has grown deep like the rivers."

Writer or Engineer?

WHEN LANGSTON reached Mexico, his father never mentioned college but took him directly to Toluca to live. This was the same place where he had spent his miserable summer one year before. He felt like rebelling.

By now his father had employed a new housekeeper, named Frau Schultz, who had come to Mexico from Germany. She was a pleasant, chunky woman with dull blue eyes and reddish-brown hair. Her husband had died and she had brought a ten-year-old daughter with her from Germany. She was a marvelous cook and always provided plenty of rich German food to eat.

Langston liked her very much, but had trouble talking with her because she spoke only German. Gradually, however, after a few weeks he learned to speak German fairly well.

Once more he spent a very lonesome summer in Mexico. He devoted much of his time to reading books and writing poems. Occasionally he took long horseback rides to some of the little villages in the country nearby.

Most of the time Langston's father was away trying to solve his business problems. He suffered heavy losses from revolutionists or terrorists who went about stealing or destroying property. The revolutionists stole all the cattle and sheep on his ranch. They even forced the electric company which he managed to be closed. Several times as he was riding over mountain roads on horseback, he was robbed.

One evening, he informed Langston that he was going to the ranch the next day along with a group of men. "You can go along, if you wish," he said. "You are old enough now to look after yourself if we meet any terrorists."

Langston wondered why his father wanted to go to the ranch now that all the animals had been stolen. "What good is the ranch without the cattle and sheep?" he asked.

His father looked annoyed. "The real value of the ranch will come from its timber, not its cattle and sheep," he sniffed.

Langston was puzzled by this statement. "From its timber?" he asked.

"Yes," explained his father. "The revolutionists have flooded all the mines nearby and destroyed the miners' barracks and houses. Before long the mine owners will try to open the mines again, and I can make thousands of dollars selling them timber from my ranch. They'll need timber to build new shafts to the mines and new barracks and houses for the miners."

The next morning Langston and his father joined a party made up mostly of mine owners and Mexican laborers. They rode safely on horseback through the majestic mountains and met no terrorists along the way. As they rode through one of the high mountain passes, however, they came across the bodies of three terrorists hanging from trees beside the road. These terrorists had been caught and hanged for their revolutionary activities. Langston cringed and tried to avoid looking at the dangling bodies.

The party rode on through a long and tiresome afternoon. At one point Langston's horse for some reason reared suddenly and bucked like a bronco. This unexpected action caused a few other horses to rear, and one of the mine owners was thrown to the ground. Langston jumped off his horse to help the man, who was soon able to climb back onto his saddle. "I'm all right," he said weakly, "and ready to go on."

"Are you sure?" asked Langston as he looked at the man's perspiring face.

"Yes," replied the mine owner, picking up the reins of his horse.

In the meantime Langston's father had been watching from a distance and had become annoyed by the delay. He came riding up rapidly and exclaimed, "Let's get on the way. We've wasted enough time here."

Langston put one foot in the stirrup, swung up on his horse, and rode along with the others. For hours they traveled through wild and bleak country with nothing much to see. Finally just before dark Langston and his father left the others to spend the night at the ranch.

When they reached the ranch, they pulled up at a hut with a campfire nearby. Soon an old woman who lived at the ranch served them a hot meal of tortillas and red beans. Both of them were hungry and gulped down their food raven-

130

ously. Then they lay down on blankets inside the hut and soon were fast asleep.

The next morning Langston and his father rode to the shaft of a flooded mine. There his father spent many hours talking with the owner of the mine. Together they made plans to open the mine by using timber from the ranch.

Later that afternoon Langston and his father rode back to the ranch. On the way his father first mentioned the subject of Langston going to college. "I want you to go to college to study mining engineering," he said.

This remark caught Langston completely by surprise. He didn't know exactly what kind of work a mining engineer did, or what he would have to study to become a mining engineer. He was almost sure, however, that he would have to study mathematics, and he knew that in his school work he never had been very good in mathematics. "No," he said firmly, "I don't think

I could study mining engineering. I've never been very good in mathematics."

"That doesn't matter," said his father bluntly. "You can learn anything if you make up your mind to learn it. Besides, mining is an important industry and you can make good money as a mining engineer."

"But I don't want to become a mining engineer," replied Langston.

"Well, what do you want to become, just a busboy or porter?" retorted his father.

"No," answered Langston calmly. "I want to become a writer."

"A writer!" snorted his father. "You can't make any money as a writer. If you'll consider becoming a mining engineer I'll send you to Europe to college. There's a good mining engineering school in Switzerland."

Langston drew a long breath. He could see that his father was determined and he wondered what he could say or do to avoid being sent to Switzerland. Finally he managed to explain that he wanted to go to college at Columbia University in New York City.

"No," said his father flatly. "I won't send you to school in the United States!"

Langston rode along quietly for some minutes. At last he built up enough courage to ask, "How long will I have to stay in Mexico?"

"You'll stay here until you decide to act wisely," replied his father coldly.

Langston knew by this statement that his father would require him to stay in Mexico until he was willing to abide by his wishes and orders. Before long he decided to find ways to earn money so he could pay for his own college education. In late summer he had an opportunity to tutor several students in English.

When Mexican schools opened in September, he was offered two positions to teach English, one in a private finishing school for girls and the other in a business college. Fortunately he was able to work out a schedule so that he could accept both positions. He taught classes at the finishing school in the morning and at the business college in the afternoon and evening.

Langston worked hard and saved as much money as he could. He even managed to save enough to send small amounts occasionally to his mother. In addition, he received a small monthly allowance from his father. Altogether, he had more money than he ever had had before in his life. All the while he kept planning to go to college the following year.

A few times during the year he took weekend trips to Mexico City. One weekend he went to the annual charity bullfight in Mexico City. Before the fight he watched beautiful Mexican young ladies ride around the arena in open carriages. He heard a band play patriotic Mexican music. Finally he was held speechless by the daring maneuvers of the bullfighter in the ring with the charging bull.

On Sunday morning he went with friends to the cathedral. He felt a warm feeling of contentment as he walked into the huge candlelit room. During the service he glanced at the many statues located around the walls. Then he wondered whether the bullfighter had come here to worship before he had gone into the ring with the furious bull.

When he got back to Toluca he sat down and tried to write a story about the bullfight. He could clearly recall the graceful maneuvers of the bullfighter and the furious charges of the bull. He could almost smell the sweat of the bull. He even could hear the roar of the crowd against the background of mellow music. Somehow, however, he just couldn't express the excitement of the bullfight in words.

Finally he gave up trying to write this story and turned to other subjects. He wrote two children's stories and a children's play which he submitted to *Brownie's Book*, a magazine for Negro children. The magazine published all three selections and the editor wrote him an encouraging letter on his writings.

Langston was elated to receive this letter. His success prompted him to submit his poem, "The Negro Speaks of Rivers," to the magazine *The Crisis*. He was elated to have the poem published in the June, 1921, issue.

Proudly he showed his father a copy of the magazine containing the poem. His father looked at the cover, turned to the poem, and read it slowly and thoughtfully. Then he closed the magazine and looked at the cover again.

As Langston had expected, his father offered no words of praise. Instead, he solemnly threw down the magazine, looked at Langston coldly, and asked, "How long did it take you to write that poem?" and then, "How much did the magazine pay you to publish it?"

"Nothing," replied Langston.

This response caused his father to utter a sneer of contempt. He couldn't understand how Langston could be happy about having his poem published without being paid for it.

Finally Langston's father gave up urging him to be a mining engineer. He consented to let him attend Columbia University and even agreed to give him a sufficient allowance to pay his tuition and living expenses. Almost immediately Langston registered by mail and made a down payment for a room in a dormitory. Then he made plans to leave for New York in time to enter school in the fall.

"The Weary Blues"

NEAR THE END of the summer Langston could hardly wait to leave for New York to enter Columbia University. His father had arranged for him to travel by railroad to Vera Cruz, a seaport to the east on the Gulf of Mexico. There he would board a ship which would take him on to New York. Early in September the time came for him to leave, and grimly his father waved to him as he boarded the train.

"Adios! Adios!" called Langston as he went up the steps. He had dreamed for a long time about going to college. Now it was hard for him to realize that at last he was on his way.

138

Vera Cruz in September was one of the hottest places Langston had ever been. He walked through the hot streets from the railroad station to the waterfront. For the first time in his life he saw the Gulf of Mexico, with its iodine odor of rotting seaweed and decaying fish. He stood for a while and watched the big ships swaying back and forth as they lay anchored by the soggy, dark pilings of the wharves.

Soon he boarded the ship which was to take him to New York. After the ship left, many passengers took sick and the ship was quarantined. From then on no passengers were allowed to leave at ports along the way.

At last the ship reached New York. As it approached the harbor Langston stood on board and looked at the city. He was eager to soak in all its beauty and enchantment.

In the distance tall buildings were silhouetted against the sky. Twinkling lights began to appear through the darkness of the city streets. Surely New York at twilight was the most beautiful city in the world.

Langston got off the ship with two Mexican friends whom he had met on the ship. The three of them looked at one another, wondering where to go. Señor Juarez, an old man who had come to live with his son in New Jersey, was carrying a crate of chickens. He put down the crate and suggested going to a hotel.

Juan, a young man who was on his way to Detroit, nodded his head and said, "Si, Señor, but where shall we go?"

Langston was glad to join the two Mexicans in finding a place to spend the night. Finally they hailed a taxicab and asked the driver to take them to a hotel. Along the way Juan kept looking out curiously at the people on the crowded sidewalks. "The people here must be richer than people in Mexico," he said to Señor

Juarez. "All of them are wearing shoes. Aren't there are any poor people here in New York?"

Señor Juarez sat watching his crate of chickens on the floor of the taxi. He kept shaking his head and saying, "New York is crowded with buildings. There are no open places with grass. Where can I find a place for my chickens?"

Langston heard these comments by Juan and Señor Juarez, but he was too thrilled to enter into the conversation. He was excited by the hustle and bustle of all the people coming and going in the big city. Then he looked curiously at the tall buildings where all of them either lived or worked.

Soon the taxi arrived at a hotel, and the three weary travelers registered into the same room. Juan and Señor Juarez went to sleep almost immediately, but Langston crouched by the window to look out at the crowded street below. Finally he settled down in bed and it seemed no time at all until he was awakened by the crowing of Señor Juarez's chickens.

At the first streak of dawn, he left for a Negro section of New York, called Harlem, where he planned to spend a few days before Columbia University would open. He walked down a long, dark stairs to take a subway train to this section of the city. Finally after he had ridden a few miles through a dark tunnel he came to the station where he needed to get off.

He rushed through the sliding doors of the train, out onto a platform crowded with hundreds of people, all of them black. At once he felt as if he were right where he belonged. Many months had elapsed since he had seen many black people at one time.

After pausing a moment, he followed the crowd up the steps to the street. There he found hundreds of other Negroes and felt happy all over again. Finally he registered at the

Y.M.C.A. and went out to mingle with the throngs of people on the streets.

When the time came for Columbia University to open, he went to the dormitory where he was supposed to stay. He walked up to the counter in the office and said, "I'm Langston Hughes. Can you tell me my room number?"

The lady at the counter checked notations on her chart and looked up at Langston. Her eyes fluttered as if she were slightly startled. Soon she managed to say, "I'm sorry, but we have no rooms available at this time. All the rooms were reserved long ago."

"I know," replied Langston politely. "I reserved my room long ago by mail and I sent in my down payment."

The lady seemed disturbed by this information and glanced at Langston again. Then she turned her back and made several hasty telephone calls. Minutes later she handed him a key

and said, "Here is your key, Mr. Hughes. You'll find your room down the hall on the first floor."

Langston didn't like Columbia University. It was so big that he felt as if he were going to school in a factory. He made very few friends

144

among the students and barely came to know any of his several instructors.

All his classes seemed dull and boring. He studied hard but unfortunately his instructors never explained anything in class. Consequently he came to look upon physics as an unsolved mystery and upon higher mathematics as some sort of Chinese puzzle. Strangely, he even found French difficult and uninteresting, although he had readily picked up both Spanish and German in Mexico. At last, he finished the year and was glad to have it over.

By now he was certain that he never would return to Columbia. He took a room in Harlem and started to look for work. He read all the help wanted advertisements and hoped to find a job he would like.

One day he called at a company that had advertised for an office boy. The office manager looked up at him over his glasses and shook his head. "We didn't advertise for a colored boy," he exclaimed in amazement.

Langston applied for many other jobs, but the answers were always the same. Before long he began to think that possibly his father was right. He wouldn't be able to earn a good living here because of the color of his skin.

Finally he obtained a job on a truck farm at the edge of the city. Every day he worked from sunup till dark, raising vegetables to sell in New York. His work was back-breaking, but he felt a great thrill in helping to raise vegetables to feed a great city.

In the fall when the truck farm season ended, he had to hunt for another job. This time he thought of applying for a job at one of the numerous docks along the waterfront in New York. He liked the odor of sea water and was entranced by all the excitement associated with the coming and going of ships at the docks.

From then on he spent much time exploring the waterfront. One day as he sat down to rest for a while, he thought of the beauty of the blue-green water far out at sea. He thought of the color and glamour of faraway places. Then suddenly he decided to try to get a job on a ship so that he could sail far out at sea and see some of the faraway places.

At once he began to look for a job on a ship, and soon obtained a job as deck hand on a rusty old freighter. He rushed up the gangplank and asked a sailor who was looking over the railing, "Where are we going?"

The sailor had worked on the old freighter for several years. He looked curiously at Langston as a new worker on the ship. "We're not going anywhere," he said.

"Not going anywhere?" repeated Langston. He could scarcely believe his ears. He thought that every ship had to go somewhere.

The sailor explained that the old freighter would be towed up the Hudson River and tied up for the winter. Only a skeleton crew would be kept on the ship to carry on the necessary work. Often there would be little to do.

That winter the sailors told Langston many thrilling stories about their adventures at sea. Also, much to his surprise, he found many good books to read in the ship's library. He was so busy that he only left the ship twice during the entire winter.

Part of the time he used for writing poetry, including one of his best-known poems, called "The Weary Blues." He based this poem on an old Negro piano player he had heard in Harlem. This piano player was tired and blue. He rocked back and forth as he played a jazz tune and sang a ragged song.

Langston wrote the first part of the poem readily without trouble. The words and lines seemed to fall into place just as he wanted them. He was dissatisfied, however, with the ending of the poem. He wrote and rewrote it many times and finally left it as follows:

> "I've got the Weary Blues
> And I can't be satisfied.
> Got the Weary Blues
> And can't be satisfied——
> I ain't happy no mo'
> And I wish that I had died."
> And far into the night he crooned that tune.
> The stars went out and so did the moon,
> The singer stopped playing and went to bed.
> While the Weary Blues echoed through his
>   head
> He slept like a rock or a man that's dead.

Many other ships besides the old rusty freighter were tied up in the Hudson River during the winter. One of them was an old empty ship which was supposed to be haunted. The sailors were afraid to go aboard the ship at night because of ghosts. "Why is the old ship supposed to be haunted?" asked Langston curiously.

"Well, during the recent World War, there was a mutiny aboard the ship," explained a sailor named Sully. "A fierce battle took place between the officers and sailors, and the captain and one of the sailors were killed. Ever since then the ship has been haunted."

"That's foolish," said Langston. "There are no more ghosts on that old ship than there are on any other ship."

"Oh, yes there are," replied another sailor, named Scotty. "Many people have seen ghosts walking around on the ship at night."

All the other sailors agreed, but Langston still shook his head. Finally the sailors began to banter him. "Would you be willing to spend a night all alone on the ship?" they asked.

"Why, of course," replied Langston bravely. "I don't believe in ghosts."

"I'll bet you ten dollars that you won't stay on the ship alone all night," said Sully.

"All right," said Langston calmly. "I'll take your bet and prepare to stay on the ship tomorrow night."

During the rest of the day the sailors kept retelling the story of the mutiny on the ship to frighten Langston. Each time they retold it they made it sound more frightening. They kept adding little bits here and there which they hadn't included before.

Late the next afternoon Langston took his bedding to the haunted ship. He walked about, looking for a cabin that had a good lock on the door. Finally he found one and spread out his bedding on the musty floor.

Sully and Scotty came to the ship to see where Langston was going to stay. "The saints have mercy!" exclaimed Sully. "You've picked the very cabin where the dead sailor stayed!"

"You'll surely turn white from fright tonight!" said Scotty.

"You guys get out of here so I can lock the door," retorted Langston.

"You'd better leave the door open so you can run!" warned Sully.

Sully and Scotty left and Langston locked the door of the cabin. Then he curled up on the bedding which he had placed on the floor and went to sleep. The wind outside made an eerie sound. At times it blew so hard that it rocked the old ship and made it rattle and squeak. None of these sounds kept Langston awake.

Only once during the night did he awaken. He imagined that he heard the door rattle as if someone were trying to get in. At first he wondered whether there might be ghosts on the old ship after all. Finally, he sat up on his bedding and called out, "Beat it, whoever you are, and let me go back to sleep."

The next morning Langston slept until the sun started to shine in the cabin window. Then he gathered up his belongings and walked back to his ship. All the sailors gathered around him to see what he would say and do.

Langston turned toward Sully. "You owe me ten dollars," he said with a broad grin. "Now I'll bet you ten dollars that you won't stay on the ship alone all night."

Sully wouldn't take the bet.

White Man or Black Man?

WHEN SPRING CAME, young Langston Hughes still wanted to get a job on a ship that would sail out to sea. He went to New York and soon obtained work on a ship that would take off for Africa. To him as a young man this was the most fortunate thing that could happen. Of all the places in the world where he wanted to go, Africa was his first choice.

As the ship plowed through the blue-green water of the open sea, he excitedly stood on deck and looked out at the distant horizon. A fresh, invigorating breeze brought up a salty spray from the sea and covered his face with moisture. At last he felt free, as if a grown man, on his way to explore the world.

The ship traveled slowly but safely across the Atlantic Ocean under sunny clear skies. Finally it reached Dakar, on the sandy western coast of Africa. From here it traveled southward to areas known as the Ivory Coast and the Gold Coast. Along the way it stopped at ports to unload its cargo of manufactured articles and take on a cargo of raw materials for the return trip to the United States.

Young Hughes was delighted with the beauty and color of the Ivory Coast and the Gold Coast. Everywhere he went he had experiences which he later wove into poems and short stories. He never forgot seeing the natives in colorful costumes or the big, brawny native men who loaded and unloaded the ship. He never forgot hearing the natives singing or the rhythmic beating of drums far into the night.

Once along the way the ship stopped for a few days at an English colony near the mouth of a river. Many white English-speaking people were waiting on shore for the ship to arrive. Here Hughes picked up information for writing a story, called "African Morning."

One of the English-speaking persons in the group was a teen-age light-skinned mulatto boy, named Edward. As the members of the crew walked down the gangplank to shore, this boy called to them, "Have you any English newspapers which I may have to read?"

On succeeding days while the ship was still anchored at the port, Edward often came to talk with members of the crew. He invited Hughes to visit him in his home. Proudly he led the way to a modest hut in a nearby village and said, "This is my home."

Inside the hut he introduced Hughes to his mother. She nodded and offered Hughes the only chair in the hut. Then she brought him a glass of fresh coconut juice to drink.

Hughes was surprised by how lovely Edward's mother looked in her African clothing. She sat on the floor and listened closely as Edward talked to Hughes about his father. "My father is an Englishman," he said. "He was in charge of a British bank here. He and my mother lived inside the English compound where the bank and the English government offices are located. That is where I was born."

"Where is your father now?" asked Hughes.

"Well, when he retired, he decided to go back to England," replied Edward, "but he didn't want to take us with him because of our color. Now he writes to us and sends us an allowance, but won't let us come to England."

"Are you happy here?" asked Hughes.

"No," replied Edward. "We're treated as if we don't belong here. The whites inside the compound don't like us because of our dark skin and the black people in the village don't like us because we once lived in the compound."

Hughes frowned as he listened. He could scarcely believe that Edward and his mother could be treated in this way. They were disliked by both the whites and the blacks.

As Hughes rose to leave, Edward looked at him and asked, "Will your ship go to England where my father lives? May I go with you?" In reply Hughes explained that his ship would not go to England on its way to America.

The day the ship left, Edward came to the dock to bid Hughes and the other members of the crew good-by. He looked just the same as he had on the day when the ship first had arrived. He stood sad and lonely on the dock in the midst of the happy persons around him.

Hughes visited many African villages and homes near the ports where his ship docked.

Everywhere the natives told him how they were oppressed by white people. "We have the same problem in America," he said.

The Africans refused to believe him. "How can you possibly have the same problem in America?" they asked curiously.

"Well, I'm a Negro in America, so I should know," replied Hughes.

The Africans laughed and shook their heads. They looked at his light brown skin and his straight black hair, like his grandmother's, and said, "You're not a Negro. You're a white man. You're a white man."

Hughes could scarcely believe his ears. He was stunned to have people in Africa call him a white man. A Negro member of the crew explained that the natives looked upon all people of mixed blood as white people. Most of the people of mixed blood who came to Africa were either missionaries or government workers.

"But I am not white," protested Hughes. He wanted people to know that he was a Negro.

"And you are not black like most Negroes," replied his Negro friend.

At one of the ports Hughes bought a young monkey, called Jocko. At first he had to keep the monkey in a cage most of the time, because he was wild. Finally, however, he tamed him to become an interesting pet. Then he and the monkey had many good times together.

When the voyage was over, Hughes brought the monkey to America. He decided to give him to his half-brother Kit, who now was eleven years old. He hadn't written anything about the monkey, because he wanted Kit to be surprised. At that time Kit and the other members of the family were living in McKeesport, Pennsylvania.

At New York, Hughes, happy to be back in America, boarded a train for McKeesport. On the train he carried the monkey in a big black traveling bag. His mother, stepfather, and Kit all met him at the railroad station.

After they arrived home, Hughes suddenly opened the big black bag and let the monkey out. Every member of the family was horrified and ran fast to hide. His mother threw up her arms frantically and cried, "Don't let that horrible animal loose here in the house!"

Within a few weeks all the members of the family came to like the monkey, especially Kit. Whenever Kit came into the house, the monkey would leap up into his arms. Then, if Kit tried to put him down, he would struggle and chatter angrily. Kit often carried him along the streets and many boys and girls from the neighborhood came to the house to see him.

After Hughes stayed with his family a few weeks, he returned to New York to look for another job on a ship. This time he hoped to get a job on a ship that would take him to Europe.

Soon he signed up an old freighter which was bound for Rotterdam, in the Netherlands.

The winter trip across the Atlantic Ocean was rough and frightening. The old freighter shook and groaned under the weight of the pounding sea. Big waves rolled across the deck like huge mountains tumbling down.

All the members of the crew felt relieved when they reached Rotterdam, but many were afraid to return on the decrepit old freighter. Langston decided to look for a job and stay in Europe for a while. He went to Paris and finally found a job as a dishwasher in a restaurant. Then he rented a little room not far away.

Hughes liked Paris and enjoyed wandering along the lively streets of the city. He welcomed the opportunity to meet interesting people and to visit exciting places. One evening he met a lovely Negro girl from Africa who had gone to school in England. She had read some of his poems in *The Crisis* and she knew quite a bit about America. She was an interesting girl and Hughes felt fortunate to have met her.

The girl's father was a wealthy businessman in Africa. When he heard that she was dating a dishwasher, he sent her back to England. Hughes was badly upset by her leaving and wrote a poem about her, called "The Breath of a Rose," which afterwards was set to music.

Before long the restaurant where Hughes was working went out of business. Then an Italian, named Romeo, who also worked at the restaurant, invited Hughes to go home with him to Italy. Hughes was eager to see many interesting places in Italy, so he accepted the invitation.

Romeo's mother lived in a small village beside a clear blue lake dotted with fishing boats. Hughes was the only young Negro the villagers had ever seen. At once everybody liked him. The fathers and mothers, the pretty young black-haired girls, and the dancing children all wanted to get acquainted with him.

When Hughes was ready to leave Italy, he boarded a train at Venice to take him back to Paris. During the night while he was sleeping, someone stole his wallet, which contained both his money and his passport for reentering France. Then he had to get off the train at Genoa, Italy.

At first he was frightened and wondered what he should do. He reported his loss to the American consul in Genoa, but the consul could do little to help him. Finally he decided to look for a job in Genoa and to stay for a while before going on.

As he wandered about the city looking for work, he discovered that jobs were hard to get, even for Italians. At last he rented a room in a cheap waterfront hotel and tried to make a living as a beachcomber. Each day he wandered along the waterfront, doing whatever odd jobs he could find here and there to earn a little money, but even odd jobs were hard to find.

Almost continuously as he lived and worked along the waterfront, he tried to get a job on a ship sailing for America. Time after time he applied on ships, but most of them employed only white persons as members of their crews. Finally, after weeks of waiting, he found employment on a ship with an all-Negro crew.

Now once more he was off for America, this time to stay for a while.

Sudden Rise
to Fame

WHEN YOUNG HUGHES reached Europe aboard
the old freighter, he had about $7.00 in his
pocket. When he returned to New York nearly
a year later, he had only a quarter in his pocket.
Later in life he joked about having taken his first
European trip for $6.75. On this trip he had
visited three important countries, France, Italy,
and Spain.

In New York Hughes submitted several of his
poems to Countee Cullen, a Negro poet, for crit-
icism. He also went to the office of the *The Crisis*
to inquire about the article which he had sent
from Italy. Much to his surprise, he found that

the article had already been published. Then he was doubly surprised to receive $20.00 for having written it.

While Hughes had been in Europe his mother and brother Kit had moved to Washington, D.C. At once he decided to go to Washington to live with them. Also, he faintly hoped to attend Howard University, a large Negro university which was located in Washington.

Hughes' mother and Kit met him at the railroad station. Kit had grown so much that Hughes scarcely recognized him. At first the three of them just stood and talked, but Hughes finally managed to ask where they were living in Washington. "For the time being we are living with our cousins," replied his mother.

"What cousins?" asked Hughes curiously. Somehow his mother always seemed to have cousins in all parts of the country.

"These cousins are direct descendants of Con-

168

gressman John M. Langston," replied his mother with a note of pride in her voice. "They have kindly invited us to stay with them, and now they want you to stay with them, too."

Hughes was surprised to find that these cousins were well-to-do. They made him welcome in their home, but seemed to be especially interested in building him up as an author. They introduced him to their friends as a poet and told them that he had just returned from Europe.

Hughes felt like laughing, because these cousins talked as if he had taken a luxurious trip to Europe instead of working his way there on an old freighter. Some of their society friends asked him many questions about his trip. "Did you meet any other authors in Paris?" asked an elegantly dressed lady.

"Not many," he replied. He would have liked to have told her that he spent most of his time in Paris washing dishes in a restaurant.

Frequently Hughes noticed expensively dressed persons looking curiously at his worn shirt and frayed trousers. Finally one of the men in a group asked, "Do you do most of your writing when you're just lounging around?"

"I write whenever I can," replied Hughes. "Usually I write when I'm off work."

"I thought that writing was your work," said the man. "Do you mean that you do other work besides writing?"

By now Hughes was becoming disgusted with these snobbish people. "Yes, I do other work besides writing," he said. "As matter of fact, I'm looking for a job right now."

Immediately all the men and ladies started to talk about different dignified jobs that they might help Hughes to get. "Perhaps we can find him a job as a page in the Library of Congress," said one of the men. "Or a job as an aide to a Congressman," said one of the ladies.

While Hughes and his mother were still living with their cousins, they were invited to a formal dinner to honor new Negro authors in Washington. On the day of the dinner one of the hostesses notified his mother that she shouldn't come unless she could wear formal clothes. Neither she nor Hughes attended the dinner.

Even though all the society people talked about helping Hughes get an important position, none of them ever tried. Finally he went out to look for work on his own and found a job in a laundry in the heart of the Negro district. Then he and his mother and Kit moved into a cheap little apartment close by the laundry.

Hughes loved the natural manners of the people in the Negro district in comparison with the false manners of the society people. This district was a run-down section where the Negroes, who worked hard with their hands, gathered for relaxation and fun. They ate barbecue and fish sandwiches or large pieces of watermelon to the sounds of colorful music. They laughed with gaiety, occasionally cried, told tall tales, and acted like people who were real.

Hughes tried to write poems like some of the songs which the people in the neighborhood sang. He noted that some their songs were gay, because they wanted to laugh, but that others were sad, because they wanted to cry. Somehow the people reminded him of the courageous persons whom his grandmother had told him about in her stories back in Lawrence, Kansas, many years before.

On Sundays Hughes enjoyed going to the neighborhood churches to hear the people shout and sing. He loved the sounds of the accompanying rhythmic tambourines or tinkling triangles. He liked the enthusiasm with which the people took part in the services.

After Hughes had been in Washington for a

few months, he tried to get a scholarship to attend Howard University. Officials at the university treated him kindly but could offer him no encouragement. His failure to get help left him downhearted, because he was almost certain that he couldn't earn enough money to pay his way through college.

During the coming months, he spent much time writing poetry. Somehow he always wrote better when he was unhappy. One of the poems which he wrote at this time, called "Dreams," starts with these lines:

Hold fast to dreams
For if dreams die
Life is a broken-winged bird
That cannot fly.

That winter Hughes caught a bad cold, which forced him to take off from working at the laundry for a week. When he returned, he found that the laundry had hired someone to replace him. Now once more he was out of work and had to look about the city for a job.

Soon through the help of a family friend he obtained a position in the Association for the Study of Negro Lives and History. Here he assisted Dr. Woodson, who was working on a book entitled *Thirty Thousand Free Negro Heads of Families*. Hughes' task was to put the thirty thousand names in alphabetical order.

This work was looked upon as a responsible position rather than as a lowly job such as he had had at the laundry. He earned more money than he had earned at the laundry, but he had to work longer hours. Often he didn't reach home until nine o'clock at night.

He realized that he was doing very important work for Dr. Woodson. Before long, however, his eyes became inflamed from reading the fine print. Then he had to give up this important position and go back to a lowly job again.

Before long he obtained a job as a busboy at the Wardman Hotel in Washington. His job was to keep the tables set with clean tablecloths and silverware and to clear away dirty dishes from the table. Taking this job turned out to be a very fortunate step.

One noon as Hughes was clearing dirty dishes from a table, he saw Vachel Lindsay, the poet, enter the dining room. He recognized Mr. Lindsay from pictures which he had seen in the morning paper. That night the poet was to give a program of reading his poems in one of the auditoriums in the hotel.

As Hughes stacked the heavy, dirty dishes, he wished that somehow he could hear Mr. Lindsay read his poems. He knew, however, that this wish was futile because no Negroes would be allowed to enter the auditorium. Then he tried to think of a plan to meet Mr. Lindsay when he came back for dinner that evening.

That afternoon Hughes copied three of his poems, "Jazzonia," "Negro Dancers," and "The Weary Blues," neatly on sheets of paper and placed them in the pocket of his white jacket. Then that evening he watched for Mr. Lindsay and quietly followed him to his table. Quickly he pulled the three poems from his pocket and laid them beside Mr. Lindsay's plate. "I like your poems, Mr. Lindsay," he said bluntly, "and hope you'll like these of mine."

Mr. Lindsay looked up with surprise. At once he picked up the three poems and started to read them. Hughes, carrying a tray of dirty dishes, shyly looked back at the table and could tell that Mr. Lindsay was highly pleased.

The next morning Hughes bought a newspaper on his way to work. He was amazed to read that Vachel Lindsay had discovered a Negro busboy poet and that he was the poet.

When he reached the hotel, he found a group

of newspaper reporters waiting to interview him. They shoved him this way and that and asked him all sorts of questions. Newspaper photographers took several pictures of him, one showing him holding a tray of dirty dishes in the dining room. This photograph appeared in many newspapers throughout the country.

Later Hughes learned that during Vachel Lindsay's program, he had read the three poems which Hughes had placed on his table. All this publicity made it difficult for Hughes to continue his job as a busboy. Many people came just to stare at him, so he decided to quit.

Shortly afterwards he learned that the magazine *Opportunity* was conducting a literary contest, including a prize of forty dollars for the best poem submitted. He sent several poems and later decided to send "The Weary Blues." Then in a few days he received the exciting news that this poem had won the prize.

Later Hughes was invited to attend a meeting in New York City to receive his award. There he met many important people, including a noted author, Carl Van Vechten, who asked, "How many poems have you written?"

Hughes laughed and shook his head. "I don't really know," he said, "but I have been writing and saving poems for several years."

"Would you possibly have enough for a book?" asked Van Vechten.

"I think so," replied Hughes.

"Well, send them to me so I can examine them," said Van Vechten.

Back in Washington Hughes gathered up his poems and sent them to Mr. Van Vechten, who in turn recommended them to a prominent publisher, Alfred A. Knopf. Soon Hughes received a letter from the publisher saying that they had been accepted for publication. The title of his first book of poems was *The Weary Blues*.

One day when he was riding on a streetcar, he noticed that a man across from him was reading a copy of a newspaper called the *Chicago Defender*. Every now and then the man looked up from the newspaper and stared at him. Finally he blurted out, "Are you Langston Hughes?"

Hughes laughed and replied, "Yes, I am, but why do you ask?"

The man held up the newspaper and pointed to a picture of Hughes with an announcement of his new book, *The Weary Blues*. Then he said, "I am Waring Cuney and I write poetry, too."

"I'd like to read some of your poems," said Hughes as the two started to talk.

Later Mr. Cuney came to show Hughes some of his poems. While they were talking, he explained that he was a student at Lincoln University near Philadelphia. "I hope to attend Howard University here," said Hughes, "but I can't get enough money for tuition."

"Why don't you plan to attend Lincoln University?" asked Waring enthusiastically. "You'll find that it is a very fine college."

After this conversation, Hughes kept thinking about Lincoln University, wondering whether he could arrange somehow to go there. Then during the Christmas season of 1925, he had a happy surprise. He received a letter from a lady whom he had met at a literary meeting in New York. In this letter she offered him a scholarship to Lincoln University. This surprise letter was the greatest Christmas gift he had ever received in his life.

This lady had enjoyed reading Hughes' poems and was eager to encourage him to keep on writing. He accepted the scholarship and entered Lincoln University at the beginning of the second semester. This time he was determined to finish his college education.

Author, Lecturer, Traveler

LINCOLN UNIVERSITY was located forty miles from Philadelphia in eastern Pennsylvania. The buildings on the campus were surrounded by grassy lawns and huge trees. The nearest village was a small settlement of a dozen homes and a tiny store about four miles away.

The university had been established to educate young Negroes in the North. All the students were Negroes, but strangely all the members of the faculty were white and the members of the board of trustees were white. No graduates had ever been invited to join the faculty or the board of trustees.

182

All the students at the university lived in dormitories. They spent most of their time during the evening studying and most of their time during the day attending classes and other school activities. As in most universities, they played many pranks on the side.

During the warmer months of the year, the students often engaged in water fights. They used the fire buckets in the dormitories to drench their fellow students. Sometimes they even doused a member of the faculty if he happened to walk near one of the dormitories.

During the winter months, the students often engaged in snowball fights. They hid behind trees and pelted unsuspecting classmates. Now and then they pelted a member of the faculty if there was no danger of being caught.

All new students at the university were hazed. For several months they were paddled nearly every night. In addition, they were required to perform many foolish activities, such as pushing pencils across the floor with their noses, dressing up like girls, or writing crazy notes to important people.

After a few months Hughes joined a fraternity at the university. He thought that the members would let him off easy in the initiation since he was a well-known poet. Instead, they made his initiation all the harder and beat him so hard that he could scarcely walk. "Take this for being a poet," they said as they whacked him.

Early the next summer Hughes was asked to read some of his poetry during commencement week at Fisk University in Nashville, Tennessee. He was pleased with the opportunity to visit this noted old Negro school in the South. He felt a great thrill of excitement as he stood and read his poems to hundreds of Negroes like himself. Somehow his poems seemed to capture many of their hopes and disappointments.

While Hughes was at Nashville, he decided to explore other parts of the South. He took a train for Memphis, Tennessee, along with a group of Negroes from Fisk University. They sat in a dusty Jim Crow car and Hughes had to put on smoked glasses to protect his eyes from cinders that came in through the open windows.

At one of the stations, Hughes and the other Negroes got off for a breath of fresh air. Then suddenly one of his Negro friends tapped him on the shoulder and said, "You'd better take off those smoked glasses. White folks don't allow Negroes to wear them here." Quickly Hughes snatched off his glasses, and everybody laughed.

After Hughes left Memphis he visited several other cities in the South and finally reached New Orleans. Soon after he arrived he found a room on Rampart street, the leading Negro street in the city. One day he walked down to the dock to watch a big ship unload bananas from the

West Indies. Soon he noted a small, dirty freighter tied up at the next pier. At once he felt homesick for a job on a boat again. Impulsively he called to a steward on board the ship, "Hey, do you happen to need a mess boy?"

The steward invited Hughes to come on board, and at once Hughes obtained a job as mess boy on a short trip to Havana, Cuba, and back. This short boat trip was just what he wanted, because he would get back in ample time to return to school in the fall.

During Hughes' junior year at Lincoln University, he began to write a novel, *Not Without Laughter*. He planned to make this novel the story of a young Negro boy, like himself, who grew up in Kansas. At first he worked very slowly on the story because he wanted it be as realistic as possible.

He worked on the novel through the summer vacation and into his senior year at college. Finally during the winter he submitted it to a publisher and it was accepted. Unfortunately, however, it never became popular and he never attempted to write a novel again.

After Hughes graduated from Lincoln University, he decided to spend his life writing, lecturing, and traveling. By now he was earning a small income from his writings and had frequent invitations to lecture on university campuses and before literary groups. Most of all, however, he wanted to travel.

One year he made a trip completely around the world. First he joined a group of actors who went to Russia to make a motion picture. The group broke up and he decided to travel on eastward across Asia. He visited several countries including China and tried to live as close to the people as he could. On the way home from Asia he stopped for a short time in Japan.

When Hughes spoke to students in his lectures, he told them that good writing would come out of their own lives. He summed up this thought by saying, "You will find the world in your own eyes, if they learn how to see; in your own heart if it learns how to feel; and in your own fingers if they learn how to touch."

Most of Hughes' poems and other writings were about people who attracted his attention for one reason or another. Generally he wrote about whole groups of people, as people in the ghetto, people in poverty, people suffering from color-line prejudices. He was proud to be an American and proud to be a Negro. Even though he had white, Indian, and Negro ancestors, he was proudest of being a Negro.

One of the best poems which Hughes wrote on the subject of color was "Dream Variations." This poem starts off like a song of dancing till the white day is done. Then darkness comes and the poem ends with the soothing lines:

188

Rest at pale evening . . .
A tall, slim tree . . .
Night coming tenderly
Black like me.

In all of his writings Hughes tried to portray the good in people regardless of race or color. Even though he was a Negro, he learned early not to hate all white people just because they were white. On the subject of color, he explained that most people were good in every country that he had visited in the world. In his poem "Daybreak in Alabama," he portrays his love for all people in these lines:

And I'm gonna put white hands
And black hands and brown and yellow hands
And red clay earth hands in it
Touching everybody with kind fingers.

Hughes wrote many poems and other writings about people he had come to know in his travels. One of the most colorful poems, "Minstrel Man," describes an old Negro entertainer in Harlem, who sings his way through the world even though he suffers from many of life's problems:

> Because my mouth
> Is wide with laughter
> You do not hear
> My inner cry?
> Because my feet
> Are gay with dancing
> You do not know I die?

Hughes grew up in poverty and wrote many poems and stories sympathizing with people in poverty. One of his most popular poems on this subject is "Evening Air Blues." Four meaningful lines from this poem read as follows:

> This mornin' for breakfast
> Chawed de mornin' air.
> But this evenin' for supper
> I got evenin' air to spare.

In all his poems and other writings, Hughes

attempted to portray people honestly and realistically. He felt that by being honest and realistic he could help people break down many barriers that existed among them. Once he said, "I try to break down barriers with my poetry."

Hughes constantly made a special plea for democracy in America and the world. He had a strong faith in the real goodness of the human heart. He always had confidence that a goal of love and peace could be realized. In his opera "Troubled Island," he expressed this peaceful dream in these words:

> I dream
> A world where man
> No other man will scorn;
> Where love will bless the earth
> And Peace its path adorn.